ONE

To Lorna Beveridge
Class P5
Room 8
Wester Overton
Primary School
1978 - 79

This Armada book belongs to:

_____

_____

_____

ONE DAY EVENT

JOSEPHINE PULLEIN-THOMPSON

Armada

First published in this edition in the U.K., 1972 by
William Collins Sons & Co. Ltd., London and Glasgow.
First published in Armada in 1974 by
Fontana Paperbacks,
14 St. James's Place, London SW1A 1PS

This impression 1979

© Josephine Pullein-Thompson 1954

Printed in Great Britain by
Love & Malcomson Ltd.,
Brighton Road, Redhill, Surrey.

CHAPTER ONE

HENRY THORNTON led his bay thoroughbred gelding, Evening Echo, up the ramp of the horse-box.

He felt harassed. The wretched horse-box driver had arrived twenty minutes late; he hoped they would be in time. Mercifully Echo was obliging about boxes; he walked straight in as usual, but he was fresh and would need a lot of riding round before his test. I hope Noel manages to get there, thought Henry. It was dreary going by oneself. He wouldn't know any of the dressage people, and anyway, it was ages since he had seen Noel. It was nearly seven months, he calculated, since last summer holidays when they had run the Radney Riding Club together. This summer he was going to insist that Uncle George had him to stay at Folly Court. He says he's not going abroad, thought Henry, so he'll have time to teach me some more dressage.

It took Noel four and a half hours to reach Mantwick. Having travelled on two buses and a stopping train, she began to wish that she hadn't been so cowardly about asking Major Holbrooke for a lift. The schedule had announced him as one of the Prix St. George judges and Noel had meant to ask at the Annual Competitions if he would take her, but then he had been so cross about Sonnet and she hadn't been able to summon up enough courage. I'm terribly cowardly, she thought, but anyway he would probably have lectured me about padlocks the whole way here.

When Noel saw horse-boxes and tents and knew that she had arrived her spirits rose. But the sight of Henry looking taller, older and more superior than ever, cast her down again. I don't suppose he really wanted me to come at all, she thought. He looks terribly grown up. She stood watching him. Echo was bucking and shying; he seemed very fresh.

When Henry saw Noel he stopped schooling and rode across to her. "Hallo," he said. "I'm glad you were able to come, though I think we're going to shatter you with our behaviour. Echo's feeling terribly bolshy; I've a nasty idea that he's going to buck."

Noel said, "He's looking lovely, but rather uppish."

"Uppish isn't in it," replied Henry, "and I've only half an hour left. I'd better get on with my exercising."

Echo wasn't going well and Noel came to the conclusion that it wasn't just over-freshness, he looked stiff and decidedly unco-operative; whenever Henry gave an aid he swished his tail.

As Henry's turn approached he resigned himself to doing badly. He was hot and tired and Echo was being just as difficult as when he had first arrived on the showground. "Oh, well, I haven't a reputation to lose, and my esteemed Uncle George is busy with the Prix St. George, so *he* won't see the horrible travesty."

Noel said, "I've got the most terrible needle. I do think it's unfair that I should have it for other people."

Henry grinned. "You'd better not watch, then, or you'll have it even worse as Test E approaches."

As the competitor before him made the final halt and salute, Henry handed Noel his stick. He rode in and walked round the outside of the markers until the judges rang the bell. He began to trot; at A he entered the arena. Oh, dear, he's terribly crooked, thought Noel.

As he rode the test Noel's depression increased. Everything seemed to be wrong and she had so hoped he would do well. She didn't want to watch Echo's unbalanced trot, his unwilling transitions, his sorry attempts at turns on the forehand, his dawdling walk or his crooked halts. She contemplated drinking tea in the refreshment tent, but she decided that that might hurt Henry's feelings so she watched him out. He, too, was conscious of the badness of

6

the test. When he rode back to her, he dismounted and, giving Echo a perfunctory pat, he said, "That was even worse than I expected. Do you think that I should scratch from the E?"

"Oh dear," said Noel, "I don't know. I disapprove of scratching on principle."

"Of course he might go better the second time," said Henry, his optimism returning. "It's all the walking at the beginning of that revolting N test that flummoxes me. He dawdles more and more with every step and one doesn't dare to do anything violent because of jogging.

"I think perhaps I won't scratch," he went on. "After all, it's different judges so I dare say I shan't give them nervous breakdowns and 2.40 is still decades away."

They watered and fed Echo and then they sat on Henry's mackintosh and watched the Prix St. George competitors. Noel told Henry about Sonnet. How the field gate had been left open by a picnic party and Sonnet had been found on the main road to Gunston with a long, deep cut in her quarters, and hardly an inch of her that was not scraped or cut or bruised. "It's terribly dreary," she finished, "to think of the whole summer stretching away before me and no pony to ride."

"Surely you can acquire something. The world's full of people who want tiresome horses schooled."

"They wouldn't want me to school them."

"False modesty," said Henry.

They watched in silence for a time and then suddenly Henry said, "I've just remembered; you wouldn't like to be given a handsome Anglo-Arab, would you?"

"Of course I would," answered Noel.

"Well, there's a Mrs. Exeter who hunts with the South Clareshires, and she's got several brood mares. Her daughter used to break the youngsters in and hunt them, but she got married a year or two ago and now Mrs. Exeter, who is getting on in years, finds herself landed with masses of half-broken Anglo-Arabs. She rang me up the other day and said that if I would have two of them and get them going for her, I could keep whichever I liked in exchange for my work and send back the other one. My dear mamma wouldn't hear of it and, of course, it would be rather tricky with me away during the term. The other disadvantage is the size; they're neither of them over 15.2 and, with my long legs, my next horse will have to be 16.2. However I could recommend you."

"That would be a rash act," said Noel. "I should ruin them both and then you would have to deal with a furious Mrs. Exeter. Besides, she wouldn't take any notice of your recommendation. One look at me would be enough to tell her that I was hopelessly inefficient."

"I'll have you know my recommendations are much prized in Clareshire. The Exeters aren't dressage-minded. They would consider Sonnet marvellously schooled. Would your people make difficulties?"

"No, I don't think so. Mr. Cox is very obliging about having extra horses, and Daddy's better off since his Egyptian discoveries brought him fame."

"We shall have to move quickly," said Henry. "School looms; I've only got two more days."

"I've three."

"We shall have to go to Recksworth to-morrow. Why haven't I taken my driving test? Still, there are trains. Could you catch an early one?"

"I expect so, but the Exeters are sure to say that they don't want me to have their horses," protested Noel.

"I'll ring up the moment I reach home. Unless they've found someone else, I know they'll be delighted."

During the luncheon interval Henry and Noel met Major Holbrooke. Noel, who didn't want to hear any more about padlocks, had been hoping to avoid him and Henry wasn't particularly pleased to be confronted by his uncle when his horse was going so badly.

"Hallo," said the Major, "what are you two doing here?"

"I'm competing," answered Henry, "and Noel is supporting my ebbing morale."

8

"How are you doing? Have you ridden yet?"

"Yes, I've done the novice test, but not very successfully. Echo seems to be behaving rather worse than usual."

"I shall be interested to see your marks," said the Major. "Mrs. Van Cutler is one of the novice judges and she knows a great deal about it."

"I can see that I shall have to make a quick getaway directly the E test is over," Henry observed, when the Major had gone on his way. "I don't think my marks are going to be of the sort to give horsy uncles pleasure."

Noel said, "Oh dear, I knew we should meet him, but he didn't offer to give me a lift home, that's one consolation."

When they had eaten lunch they unboxed Echo and Henry rode him round while Noel tried to make helpful remarks. It was a disheartening task because she could see that there was nothing to be done before the test; somewhere his schooling had gone wrong, but it needed weeks to correct it, not minutes.

Once again there was nothing to admire about Echo's performance in the arena. It was alternately unwilling and hurried, and the more difficult movements were very bad indeed.

When Henry came out his last shred of optimism had vanished. "That was even worse," he said quietly. "I'm hopeless. I'd better try point-to-pointing, or become a plain hunting type."

"Perhaps Echo's just in a bad mood."

"I could cheerfully shoot myself."

They boxed Echo and then drank tea, talking carefully of anything but dressage until Henry said, "Let's gather our ebbing courage and see if we can collect my novice marks yet."

The Elementary test was still in progress, but Henry was given his marks for the Novice.

"Now for Mrs. Van Cutler's esteemed opinion," he said. "Oh *lord*! Have you ever seen so many fours? 'Horse not on bit. Horse off bit. Stiff. Not cadenced. Unbalanced. Stiff.

9

Hurried. Not a true circle. Bad halt. Crooked, off bit. Running, unbalanced. The horse was never between rider's hands and legs,'" he read off the remarks. "Generous female, she's actually given me five for my loose rein walk," he observed. "Well, I'm off," he went on, "I'm not waiting for my E marks. Come on, I don't want to run into my dear uncle. My apologies for having brought you so far for such a sorry spectacle," Henry went on as they hurried towards the box, "but you have supported me in my hour of need."

"I feel rather useless," Noel confessed. "I ought to be bracing or heartening; helping you to keep a stiff upper lip. Quoting '*If*' like you did last summer."

Henry shuddered. "Don't mention it," he said. "I've quite given up feeling like that."

"Hallo, I've been looking for you two everywhere," said Major Holbrooke, appearing from the tea tent. "Noel, how did you get here? Have you transport home? Because, if not I can easily give you a lift."

"I came by bus and train," answered Noel.

"It must have taken hours," said the Major. "I'd have offered you a lift if I had known you were coming. I don't know why you didn't ring me up. Anyway, I'm going home directly all the results are out and you'll find my car behind the Prix St. George arena judges' tent. How did you do, Henry?"

Henry, concealing his marks behind his back, answered calmly, "I fear your friend Mrs. Van Cutler didn't care for me overmuch. The other judges had a low opinion of me, but hers was even lower, in fact, you had better disclaim all relationship."

The Major looked at him suspiciously. "Old Tubby Barnes shouldn't be on the judges' panel at all, but Mrs. Van Cutler's opinion is worth having—she knows."

"Oh dear," said Henry, "then only two courses are left open to me. Either, Uncle George, you have me to stay in the summer holidays and school me madly, or else I become a hunting type, sitting well back and spending nonhunting days writing letters to the sporting press on how dressage ruins good horses."

"You can come to stay if you want to, though why you people can't school your horses is beyond my comprehension. It's just the same with our Pony Club; if I take my eye off them for five minutes they've gone to pieces."

"Can I come right at the beginning of the holidays?"

"Yes, I suppose so, if you don't make a nuisance of yourself."

"Thank you, Uncle George. You've no idea what you've done for me. Hope is restored."

"Well, I'll see you later at the car, Noel. Good-bye, Henry." Major Holbrooke left them.

"Lord, I was afraid that he was going to demand to see his dear Mrs. Van Cutler's frank opinion," said Henry, when his uncle was out of earshot.

"Oh dear," wailed Noel, "I *know* he's going to lecture me on padlocks the whole way home and when anyone mentions Sonnet I feel like giving six sharp screams."

"You mustn't be so temperamental," said Henry. "Anyway, he won't; he's forgotten all about that by now, and if he does you'll be able to use Mrs. Van Cutler's remarks to change the conversation, once I'm safely away. When he says, 'You can get them for about 37½p at Flapton's,' you can quickly interpose, 'Fancy, Henry only got four for his first circle; Mrs. Van Cutler thought Echo stiff, unbalanced and off the bit.' "

"I wouldn't be so mean, but I can't help being temperamental when everyone keeps on and on about Sonnet as though I wasn't already fed up at having her full of stitches and nothing to ride all summer."

"Well, I'm dealing with that problem," said Henry, "don't forget my two delightful Anglo-Arabs."

To Noel's surprise the Major didn't mention padlocks the whole way home. After a short discourse on the rising standard of dressage he asked what she was proposing to do about a mount and, on hearing Henry's plan, he became

11

quite enthusiastic. "Just the thing for you," he said, "because, of course, you won't be able to ride Sonnet in adult tests, they're all for horses. I'll tell you what I'd do with her, if she were mine," he went on, "I'd breed from her now, while she's lame. Send her to a thoroughbred; you might get a very nice little horse of hack type." And when he left Noel at Russet Cottage he added, "If you do decide to breed from her, let me know. You can turn her out with my brood mares, then she'll have company and one more won't make any difference to me."

Noel was overcome. "Thanks awfully," she said. "That's terribly nice of you," and she was haunted by remorse for having made such a fuss about one lecture on padlocks. She said good night to the Major and thanked him for the lift, and then she dashed into Russet Cottage to tell her parents all her hopeful news before going out to settle Sonnet for the night and put penicillin in all her numerous wounds.

CHAPTER TWO

"DON'T be absurd, Henry," said Mrs. Thornton at dinner on the first evening of the summer holidays. "Of course you can't go to Folly Court with your uncle and aunt still in the nursing home. Everyone there will have quite enough to do without you adding to their worries. You'd better come to Scotland with Elizabeth and me."

"I'd rather stay here with Papa," answered Henry. "I know you think I'm a burden, but I *can* be quite useful. I can ride most of Uncle George's horses without falling off; I know most of Aunt Carol's birds. Anyway, I think some-one ought to go to Folly Court, and as my dear cousins are in foreign parts, it's practically my duty to go."

"And if you go careering off to interfere in your uncle's affairs, who's going to ride Echo?"

"I'll take him with me," answered Henry. "Uncle George won't mind. Think how cheered he'll be, as he lies in his dreary nursing home, to get reassuring letters from his fond nephew. None of the staff at Folly Court are cap-able of writing a letter, except Nanny, and everyone knows that she lies if it suits her, or if you're ill and she thinks you ought not to be worried."

West Barsetshire was horrified by the news of the train smash, and the first reports of the Holbrooke's injuries were particularly alarming. The subscribers to the Hunt, the Pony Club members and all the Holbrookes' personal friends telephoned Folly Court for news. But, owing to Nanny's aversion to the telephone, and the fact that the Lithuanian married couple knew only a few words of English, no one learned more than: "Major Holbrooke away. Him very bad. Mrs. Holbrooke away, her very bad too," and they all went un-reassured.

Henry was surprised by the warmth of the welcome he received from everyone. Nanny, who had moved into the Court from the Lodge because she suspected that the Lithuanians would make off with the silver, insisted that Henry should inhabit the best guest room. Blake, the Major's stud groom, brushed aside all suggestions that Echo would be a nuisance.

"Of course 'e won't, Mr. 'Enry. One more won't make no difference. What we want is someone to 'elp with the exercising. Fred, 'e 'asn't been feeling too grand lately, and Ariel and Apollo—they're South Wind's two colts—they've 'ad 'im off a time or two and 'e's packed it up. Won't ride 'em no more. They've 'ad Victor off as well, but 'e don' worry so much. Then there's 'Armony, well the Major, 'e don't like 'er ridden by anyone else, so I lunges 'er. The old show-jumpers and the 'Unt 'orses are all turned out, but there's Doomsday, 'e's a Grade C 'orse the Major bought two or three months back, and there's the Merry Widow, she's all right, and then there's that chestnut, Spartan. 'E's an 'orrible 'orse, 'e is. Kick you as soon as look at you, 'e would. I don't know what the Major's going to do with 'im, I'm sure. They're not getting enough exercise, that's the trouble, but my riding days are over, and there's plenty of work with the mares and foals."

Henry said, "Yes, you certainly seem to have plenty to do. Of course, Uncle George reckons to do a good deal of exercising when he's at home. Still, I'll do what I can."

Henry felt very elderly sitting down to lunch by himself with Stefan, in a white coat, waiting on him. Nanny came in to tell him that the telephone had been "ringing and ringing," but that she wasn't going to answer; she couldn't make head nor tail of what it said.

"Can't Stefan or Mrs. Stefan answer it?" asked Henry.

"Whatever's the good of sending an ignorant foreigner like that to answer it?" asked Nanny acidly. "They don't understand English and no one can understand a word they say. You might as well bring in your poor aunt's parrot and let 'im answer it."

14

Henry said, "Well, when I'm in I'll answer it and when I'm out it'll just have to ring."

After lunch he telephoned Noel. She was very surprised to hear that he was at Folly Court, but he wouldn't tell her anything about why or how he was there. "Come over to tea. Four-thirty," he said, "and you shall hear all."

Noel found Henry in the saddle room, cleaning tack. He looked hot and dishevelled with his fair hair hanging down over his face.

"Gosh! What unusual energy."

"I feel very virtuous," he said, looking up. "But I've nearly finished and then we'll have tea."

"Folly Court seems terribly deserted," said Noel, "what's happened to everyone?"

"Blake and Victor are turning out the mares, Fred's gone home—he's feeling queer. Everything's in the most terrible muddle; half the horses haven't been exercised. I can't think what Uncle G. would say if he knew."

"How are the Major and Mrs. H.?" asked Noel. "No one around here really knows how bad they are."

"They're both getting on marvellously now. Aunt Carol has a broken wrist, cracked ribs and shock—but she's over the shock and the broken wrist is in plaster and the ribs will take about another fortnight. Uncle G.'s in the worse state. He had concussion and he was unconscious for several hours so he's got to stay in bed now, to avoid going dotty later. He's got a broken arm too, and I gather it was a bit of a mess."

"Oh dear, and it's beastly for them right in the middle of summer. The Major won't be able to jump for ages, I suppose, and I did want some advice."

"Advice on your Anglo-Arabs?" Henry asked.

"Yes. They're quite quiet to ride now, at least they're as quiet as you'd expect; they buck and shy a bit, but they're broken in. The trouble is that I don't seem to get anywhere with my schooling. I'll bring them over to-morrow and see what you think."

15

"Echo being such a wonderful advertisement for my methods and knowledge," said Henry sarcastically. "Come on, I've finished my chores and I'm dying for tea. One thing about Folly Court," he went on, as he led the way to the house, "you're wonderfully fed. Uncle G. and Aunt Carol don't believe in plain living and high thinking like my esteemed mamma."

Henry and Noel took it in turns to answer the telephone during tea. Every time it was someone inquiring after the Holbrookes, and the inquirers were so pleased to find someone who knew the latest facts that they talked on and on. Noel and Henry had no time to converse with each other at all for no sooner was one caller satisfied than the telephone rang again.

"I'm going to teach Stefan a reassuring sentence," said Henry in exasperation as the telephone rang again and Noel said that it was his turn and that she must go home.

"Well, look," said Henry, ignoring the ringing phone, "bring your steeds over to-morrow morning, as early as you can, and we'll provide each other with moral support."

"O.K.," said Noel. "You'd better answer it. Good-bye, and thanks awfully for my nice tea."

Noel had never tried to lead Truant from Tranquil before and she arrived at Folly Court cross and exhausted, the two horses having shied, bumped into each other and proceeded in fits and starts the whole way.

Henry was saddling Spartan. "Hallo. More trouble," he said. "Fred's been taken to hospital with an appendix. This doesn't seem to be Uncle George's lucky year."

"Poor Fred, no wonder he was feeling queer."

"It's a good thing I came," observed Henry. "Even my dear mamma would have to admit that now. Victor could never cope with all the exercising by himself. Look, do you mind coming out for a hack first? I don't aspire to schooling Uncle George's horses. Bag a box for whichever one of yours you're not riding."

Noel decided that she would hack Tranquil and she put Truant in a loose box. Henry wanted to go round by Lower Basset Farm; he was curious to see John Manners' new horse, Samson.

"He's an ugly horse," Noel told him, "but I should think he would make a good hunter. He's about sixteen-two, a nondescript bay with a terrific Roman nose."

"John needs something up to weight," said Henry, mounting Spartan. "He was huge last summer. He's not as tall as me but he's miles broader."

When Spartan reached the end of the drive he said that he had gone far enough. He stopped dead, rolled his eyes, and when Henry tried to send him on he took his forelegs off the ground, threatening a rear.

"Shall I go first?" offered Noel.

"O.K.," Henry answered, "but I expect I shall have to have it out with him sooner or later."

Tranquil, who was generally obliging, decided that Spartan had seen some dreadful danger lurking in the road, so he said that he was afraid and began to go back-wards, bumping into Spartan. Both the horses retreated up the drive, clinging to each other and making it very diffi-cult for their riders to use their legs or sticks.

"For heaven's sake, Noel, get out of the way," said Henry. "I want to wallop this wretched animal."

"Sorry," said Noel, "if you can stand still a sec, I'll try." She turned Tranquil and rode back towards the Court. Henry hit Spartan, who swung round with a rear. Henry turned him and hit him again. Spartan bucked. Henry went on hitting him every time he bucked until suddenly Spartan walked quietly forward into the road. Tranquil followed immediately.

"It's simply that he wants his own way," said Henry. "He is a wretch. He wasn't frightened at all. I reckon he's been having jolly fun with poor Fred."

"Tranquil's not on the bit," said Noel drearily. "I do wish I could get him to use his hocks properly."

Spartan had another jibbing fit when he was asked to go

17

into the yard at Lower Basset Farm, but this time he gave in quite quickly. There was no one about in the farmyard and no sign of Samson or Turpin, so they took the cart track which led along the valley and met John Manners driving a tractor and trailer. The horses at once refused to go forward. They said that the tractor was dangerous. Spartan bumped into Tranquil, who tripped in a rut. John throttled down the engine. "Hallo," he yelled, "how's the Major?"

"Much better," shouted Henry, quarrelling with Spartan. "He's coming on well. We came to see your new horse," he added, as Spartan consented to pass the tractor. Tranquil followed, trembling and snorting.

"He's up over the hill, out with the cows. I'll bring him over to see you at the end of the week. Got to get this wretched barley in," roared John.

"O.K.," said Henry, as the horses, astonished at their own bravery, fled down the cart track.

"He looks just like a farmer," said Henry, when they were under control again.

"Yes, it's all terribly satisfactory," said Noel, "because his parents wanted him to farm and he likes it, though he's always swearing about the harvest or something. I do wish I knew what I wanted to do."

"I'm going into the Army," said Henry, "the Horse Guards, if they'll have me. You see the world and they like one to ride."

When Noel and Henry, weary from quarrelling with their bad-mannered mounts, returned to Folly Court, they found Susan Barington-Brown in a great state of excitement.

"Oh thank goodness you've come," she said. "That tiresome Truant jumped out of his box and all the other horses got excited and the grey ones went nearly mad. I thought I was going to have the whole lot out. I managed to get him back and I've shut the top door, but he's still tearing round like a mad thing."

"Oh dear," said Noel, "I thought he'd given up jumping

18

out. I suppose it was being in a strange place. Thanks for catching him. It was lucky that you turned up."

"I went to Russet Cottage first, but your mother told me you were here."

"Heavens!" said Henry, looking at his watch. "It's half-past eleven. I'm going to school Echo. I wonder if Spartan's tack will fit him?"

"Are you going to school, Susan?" asked Noel.

Susan answered that if both the others were going to, she supposed she might as well.

The schooling was even less successful. Truant began by bucking Noel off and galloping round and round the school, upsetting Echo, who gave one of his bucking and kicking displays and very nearly had Henry off too. At last Noel managed to catch Truant and Susan held him while she remounted. But though he didn't buck her off again, both he and Echo saw imaginary evil in the hedges which surrounded the school. Every so often one of them shied or shot into a gallop and then, directly their superfluous energy wore off, they began to dawdle. Echo overbent and Truant drooped.

Susan was the only cheerful person. She chattered gaily. "Wonder's turns are much better. She only needed a little practice. Of course it's absolutely *ages* since I schooled her. I don't suppose there'll be a Pony Club Team this year with the Major ill. We had such fun last year. I wish you'd been in it, Noel, but then of course I probably wouldn't have been in myself."

"I don't think there would have been a team this year if the Major hadn't had an accident," said Noel, abandoning her attempts at shoulder-in. "He seemed rather fed up with us all."

"Oh, that doesn't mean a thing," Susan told her. "He's always threatening that he won't do this or that, but in the end he always does."

Henry said, "It's a quarter to one; we'd better stop."

"Oh dear, Truant hasn't improved a bit," moaned Noel.

"Well, Echo gets worse and worse," said Henry in disagreeable tones, "so if your hopelessness is stationary you're considerably better off than I am."

"Goodness!" Susan exclaimed, "I must go. Shall I come up to-morrow and help clean tack or something?"

"If you can spare the time," answered Henry.

"You'll lunch here, Noel, won't you?" said Henry when Susan had gone. "I told Nanny you would."

Noel answered that she would love to, but that she must ring up her family.

After lunch they decided to lunge Ariel and Apollo. They lunged them for twenty minutes and then Henry led Noel round the school on each of them in turn. Noel insisted on riding because she said that if they bucked and she was leading she would be certain to let go.

At half-past three they began to clean tack in gloomy silence. Noel broke it. "Are you in despair?" she asked.

"Yes, and not without good reason."

"Do you think," she suggested tentatively, "that lunging would do us good? Your Uncle George is always saying that no one can get far in dressage with a bad seat, because you can't drive and all the rest of it, and lunging is supposed to improve one's seat. I read that at the Spanish School of Vienna they lunge you for three months, and our Olympic team was lunged."

"Yes, I heard that too," said Henry. "One would feel an idiot going round and round, but still, I suppose if they could do it—I'm in the mood to clutch at straws."

"I wanted to try it in the term," Noel told him, "but Susan thought I was mad and wouldn't co-operate. Tranquil would be quiet enough," she went on, "but I wouldn't fancy Truant without stirrups or reins."

"Echo will be jolly. Still, one can knot the reins and grab them if the 'orse starts any funny stuff or the lunger lets go."

"Shall we start to-morrow?" asked Noel.

"I don't see why not."

Noel arrived at Folly Court less exhausted by riding one and leading one at the second attempt.

She found the yard littered with brooms, pitchforks and pieces of straw. "I seem to be a perpetual bearer of bad news," Henry said. "Blake got kicked by Spartan just after you left last night. His leg doesn't seem to work this morning so he's gone to get himself X-rayed."

Noel said, "The fates do seem against Folly Court at the moment."

"Victor and I have mucked out rather hastily and haphazardly," Henry told her. "Now he's gone to get the mares and foals in and I'm trying to sweep up."

"I'll come and help," said Noel.

The yard was restored and Noel and Henry had started to groom when there was the clatter of hoofs and most of the Radcliffe family appeared in the yard.

"Hallo," yelled the Radcliffes, "we've come to help."

"We heard from Susan that you were here," Roger explained, "and then Doc told us about Fred and Blake so we thought you might be glad of some extra labour."

"It's very thoughtful of you," said Henry, "but what on earth are we going to do with all these steeds?"

"What about the barn?" asked Hilary. "We used it quite a lot at Pony Club rallies last year."

"We've brought halters and lunches," said Evelyn. As the redheaded Ratcliffes rode to the barn, Noel asked Henry, "What are we going to find for them to do?"

"There's masses of grooming still,' said Henry, "and I don't see why they shouldn't help with the exercising. Hilary and Roger ride just as well as Fred. Margaret and James can fill haynets."

The elder Radcliffes were very efficient. They groomed Ariel, Apollo and Doomsday and the Merry Widow while Noel did Harmony, and Henry Spartan and Echo.

"What now?" said Evelyn briskly.

"Well," said Henry, "we've got to exercise and Noel and I were proposing to lunge each other," he added self-consciously.

"Lunge each other? Whatever for?" asked Evelyn.

21

"We have our reasons," Henry said. "Shall we get it over first, Noel?"

"Yes, but I don't like the idea of an audience."

"Oh, you must let us watch," said Hilary.

Neither Noel or Henry wanted to be lunged first so they tossed up and Henry won.

"Oh dear," said Noel, "how mean. I wish I'd never suggested it, and I'm sure Tranquil's going to buck."

"Well, the school's nice and soft," said Henry, arming himself with a lunge whip. "Come along, no repining."

Noel put on her crash cap and fetched Tranquil. She mounted, pulled the stirrups off the saddle, and put a knot half-way up the reins.

"This *is* going to be fun," said Evelyn. Margaret said "Oh, Noel, you are mad, honestly."

"When I've got the most wonderful dressage seat and Truant and Tranquil go like Harmony you'll all be jealous," said Noel.

"Oh, I do hope he bucks," said Margaret, as Henry told Tranquil to walk on.

"What's it like?" asked Henry.

"Restful," answered Noel. "I'm relaxing. It's lovely having no reins and not having to use one's legs."

"Trot on," said Henry. "Beast," said Noel. "This is awful. You're not supposed to grip. You're supposed to put your knees down as far as they'll go and then stay on by your weight and the laws of gravity."

"Is that holding on allowed?" asked Henry suspiciously.

"Yes, definitely. You've got to prevent yourself slipping back to the cantle somehow," said Noel breathlessly, "but you're not supposed to hold on all the time."

"Do you want to go round the other way yet?"

"I want to walk. I shall fall off in a minute if I don't."

Henry called Tranquil into the centre and then sent him round the opposite way. "You've only had five minutes," he told Noel, looking at his watch.

"Your watch must have stopped."

"It hasn't."

"Well, the article I read said that you were to be lunged for half an hour twice a day," said Noel in tones of horror.

"Tough lot, the Austrians," observed Henry. "Stop gossiping; it's time you did some more trotting."

After a few minutes Noel asked, "Do you think I look any better? You must criticise me or it's no use."

"You don't look bad," answered Henry, "except that your eyes are firmly fixed on the ground."

Noel groaned. "I'd forgotten about looking up," she said, "I'm sure it *must* be your turn now."

"It isn't, you've only had eight minutes; you really are a most unpersevering character."

When Noel's ten minutes were up, Henry said he thought he might as well ride Tranquil too. Noel agreed and he vaulted on while she took over the whip and rein. "Now then, teacher, elucidate," said Henry. "I've no idea what I'm supposed to do."

"Well, nor have I," said Noel, "at least not really; I can only tell you what I remember. You sit in the lowest part of the saddle on the bottom of your spine. You sit up terribly straight. Then you make your legs as long as possible, without stiffening them, and your knees should be very low."

"What about my toes?"

"Oh, they just hang naturally, but you mustn't turn them out too much or you might start gripping with the back of your leg." Henry arranged himself carefully. "There," he said. "Have I the perfect seat?"

"It's much better," answered Noel, looking at him critically, "but you still look rather on top of the saddle. Can't you get your knees a bit lower and your seat bones a bit farther forward?"

Henry made a despairing face. "I already feel as though I were on the rack," he answered. "There, that's as low as my knees will go at the moment. What about a trot?"

Tranquil trotted and Henry bounced.

"This is terrible," he said. "One has to hang on for grim death to stay in the right place."

"Your knees are creeping up," said Noel.

"It's much easier with them up. How long have I had now?" he asked after a few moments.

"Four and a half minutes," answered Noel. "I don't see how we're ever going to stand half an hour."

The Radcliffes were finding the lunging very dull. Margaret and James had discovered some burrs, which they were throwing at each other.

"I should like to know the point of this," said Roger.

"It's all done so that they can shine at dressage tests," Evelyn told him, "weeks of work just to be able to go round one silly little square better than anyone else."

"But there aren't going to be any tests held round here this summer," said Hilary.

"They'll probably go miles to find one," Evelyn answered, "they're mad enough for anything."

Just as Henry's turn came to an end there was a clatter of hoofs in the yard and Christopher Minton's head appeared over the hedge.

"Hallo," he said. "What's going on?"

"Hallo," said the other Pony Club members, and Henry added: "We're just coming in." He dismounted stiffly

They led Tranquil to the yard.

"I came to inquire how the Major was," Christopher told them. "I had no idea that all you lot were here. I presume the Major's still away."

"Yes, he's still in the nursing home," Henry answered, "but both he and Aunt Carol are getting on well now. They've finished putting nuts and bolts in Uncle George's arm, so I should think they'll let them come home fairly soon, but he won't be able to ride for ages."

"Does that mean there won't be any rallies these holidays?" asked Christopher. "I'm not going if it's only Miss Sinclair taking them."

"Oh, I shouldn't think there's much hope of Uncle George instructing," answered Henry. "He was being a bit bolshy about the Pony Club before the train accident—wasn't he, Noel?"

"Yes, that's right," agreed Noel. "He seemed a bit fed up with us."

"I don't altogether blame him," said Christopher. "Look at people like John and Susan. He's spent weeks on them and they never get any better. But it's a bit hard on the people who want to get on; perhaps he could take two or three of us for some really advanced dressage."

"Not me then," said Henry, "I'm not advancing another inch until I can ride the Novice test properly."

"Well, surely you can do that now," objected Christopher. "There's nothing in it. It's no more difficult than the Pony Club test we did last summer."

"Nothing in it?" said Henry. "I thought it tested the whole basic training of the riding horse."

"Well, you know what I mean," said Christopher, reddening, "It's all very elementary stuff."

"Which horses are we going to exercise next?" asked Noel. "Lunch-time is rapidly approaching."

"Well, if some of these people would like to ride Doomsday and the Widow that would save Victor and he could lunge Harmony. We can ride Spartan and Truant now and Ariel and Apollo after lunch."

"I'll ride Doomsday," shrieked Margaret.

"Oh no, you won't," Henry told her.

"I'll ride Doomsday," said Christopher, "and one of the Radcliffes can have the Widow. Bags the Major's Italian saddle."

The Radcliffes decided that Hilary should ride the Merry Widow and that the rest of them would come on their own horses and ponies "to collect the corpses."

Noel felt rather apprehensive. "I hope that you're going to be able to control everyone," she said to Henry. "It's rather nerve-racking having so many of the Major's horses out in such a rabble."

"I can control the people," answered Henry. "It's Spartan over whom I have no influence whatever."

As the cavalcade of horses left the stableyard Susan came riding down the drive on Wonder.

"Goodness," she said, "what a huge party. Where are you going? Can I come too?"

Everyone said yes, and Henry added that they were going for a sedate ride with only one canter and that those who wanted to gallop could buzz off as he wasn't going to have his uncle's horses lamed on the hard ground.

Susan rode with Noel who told her about Blake's accident. Christopher was riding beside Henry and telling him about the Bank Holiday Show. The Radcliffes came behind in a bunch. Spartan was a nuisance. When Henry rode him among the other horses he bumped into them, dawdled and refused to use his hocks properly; when Henry took the lead he shied every few moments, and when Henry hit him he lashed out, once only just missing Doomsday. Truant was nervous. He was afraid of being kicked by the other horses.

"Keep off my tail," shouted Henry suddenly as Spartan observed a cow in a field beside the lane and announced that he would go no farther. "He isn't frightened, he's simply jibbing." He hit Spartan, who kicked out. He went on hitting him; Spartan gave several half rears and shot up a bank and down into the lane again with a clatter, which horrified Truant, who swerved round, gave a buck, and galloped off up the lane. Henry battled with Spartan and then suddenly the horse gave in and walked past the cow quite calmly. Noel had Truant under control again, but she followed at a discreet distance.

"Here's our canter," said Henry, stopping beside a gate. "We'd better canter in some sort of order. Noel and I are the most perilous."

"I'm perfectly under control," said Christopher. "You needn't worry about me."

"Well, Noel and I'll go first and then Doomsday and the Widow, because they may get excited. And don't gallop past me or you'll probably get kicked."

Henry started off across the fields. Noel followed. Spartan was trying to shy but Henry drove him on. Noel could hear the others catching up as they began to ride downhill; Truant didn't like the sound of hoofs behind him; he began to gallop faster with his tail tucked in as though he was running away from something. And then, right at the narrowest part of the track, Spartan saw an old sack hanging on the fence and stopped dead. Truant cannoned into him. "Hold hard!" yelled Henry, but no one stopped. Christopher crashed into Truant, Hilary into Christopher. Everyone was up his horse's neck and James was on the ground.

"Are you all right?" they asked as James got to his feet. "Oh yes, perfectly," he answered, "I didn't notice that the rest of you had stopped."

"Sorry, everyone," said Henry. "It was my fault, but I haven't much control over Spartan."

"I couldn't stop Pilot. He was going hell for leather," said Evelyn, laughing.

"I didn't like to haul at the Widow's mouth."

"I was under control," Christopher told them, "but I didn't like to stop because of the people behind."

"Oh well, there's no more downhill and, I hope, no more sacks," said Henry.

Noel was secretly relieved when they returned to Folly Court without further mishap.

"You're lunching with me, aren't you?" asked Henry.

"Oh dear, I don't know. Do you think I ought? I don't want to impose on the Major's hospitality."

"Look," said Henry, "I have to eat breakfast alone, dinner alone and quite often tea alone, and I don't see why I shouldn't have someone to lunch."

"O.K.," said Noel. "I'd love to if you're sure, but I should hate the Major to think we'd made use of Folly Court for our own ends as soon as he fell ill."

"He won't and we're not," answered Henry.

The Radcliffes and Susan tied their ponies in the barn and ate their lunches in the park. Christopher said that he had to go, but he would be up to help next day.

After lunch Henry said that he would lunge Ariel and that Hilary, who had been one of the Pony Club horse-

27

breakers and was experienced, could lunge Apollo. The two greys lunged very well, but afterwards, when Hilary led Noel round the school on Apollo and Roger Radcliffe led Henry on Ariel, they were not so well behaved. They trod on their leaders' toes and gazed about and neighed in an inattentive manner. Margaret nearly had Noel off by throwing James's crash cap into the hedge as Apollo was going by. "Really, Marga, you are a fool," said Hilary when she had got Apollo under control. "Don't you know a young horse when you see one?"

"Oh, I always forget that the Major's horses are such nervous wrecks," answered Margaret impatiently. "It's do them good to have a few frights."

"I'd rather you waited until Henry and I have got off," said Noel.

"Oh, Noel, you're really too fussy for words. Surely you don't mean to say *you're* afraid of falling off?" said Margaret in a tone of voice calculated to irritate.

"Shut up, Margaret," said Susan. "Noel isn't a bit fussy; she doesn't mind falling off and she knows much more about horses than you do."

When Ariel and Apollo had had their lessons, Henry said that he felt too worn out with work and worry to ride Echo. "He'll have to exercise himself in the park," he told Noel. "It's all this lunging."

"My legs feel terrible, and the rest of me is limp like chewed string. Nothing but the most exquisite dressage seat is going to be worth so much agony," said Noel.

Soon everyone was cleaning tack and there was the usual uproar and bickering over sponges, hooks and space on the saddle horse.

"This reminds me of the summer before last when the Major had that dressage course," said Susan. "Do you remember how Christopher and Merry Hemlock-Jones used to quarrel?"

"And John and Henry," added Hilary.

"Oh, we didn't," objected Henry.

"Yes, you did," shouted all the Radcliffes at once, and

28

Susan said: "Don't you remember, you fought one evening and the Major caught you?"

"That wretched Christopher has got away with it to-day," said Henry, changing the subject. "He had a ride and didn't do a stroke of work—I'm cleaning his tack."

"He couldn't help it," said Susan. "He had to go home to lunch. He's coming over to-morrow to help properly."

"Are many people coming over to-morrow?"

"Well, I am," answered Noel.

"I'm coming," said Susan. "I think it rather fun, us running Folly Court like this."

"We're coming, aren't we?" asked Roger, looking questioningly at his sisters.

"I don't see why not," answered Evelyn.

"Well, the thing is," said Henry, "if I can be spared; if the rest of you will help Noel to hold the fort, I thought of catching the ten-thirty train to London and visiting my uncle and aunt. You see, if Uncle George isn't going to be able to ride for ages, I can't see any point in keeping so many horses up. But I daren't write and tell him about Fred and Blake for fear of throwing him into a flap. In fact, I don't think I dare tell him about Blake because I'm sure it would give him a nervous breakdown, secondary concussion and post-operational fever to think of us and Victor looking after his horses."

"We'll manage all right, won't we, Noel?" said Susan.

"I don't know," Noel spoke doubtfully, "it's a bit nerve-racking dealing with someone else's horses."

"You needn't exercise them," said Henry, "and it doesn't really matter if they're groomed, as long as they're fed and watered."

"But exercising's half the fun," objected Evelyn. "We shall be perfectly all right. Don't take any notice of Noel; you know what a fuss she always makes."

"Well, anyway, I hope Blake will be better," said Henry.

CHAPTER THREE

WHEN Noel arrived at Folly Court on Wednesday morning she found that Henry had already mucked out and groomed Spartan and Echo.

"I *must* ride Echo to-day," he moaned, rushing about distractedly. "Blake's not coming. His kneecap's cracked and Victor's in a mood. He's mucked out Doomsday and the Widow and now he's gone to fetch the mares in. I'm sorry to leave you so much to do, Noel."

"That's all right," said Noel. "I'll manage."

"I can't possibly ride Spartan as well as Echo. I know I'm going to miss that train as it is."

"Well, it won't hurt Spartan to have a day off, will it?"

"It won't hurt *him*, but he'll buck me off to-morrow."

He rode away down the drive still muttering.

There were only three boxes to muck out, thought Noel, collecting tools and the wheelbarrow; but the yard was in a terrible mess. Henry and Victor seemed to have scattered hay and straw all over it. Harmony was obliging; she moved over whenever she was asked and her box was reasonably clean. But Apollo had upset his water bucket and mixed his hay in with his bed, he stood on whichever piece of straw Noel was trying to fork, and when asked to move over he either refused to budge or moved in the wrong direction. Every time Noel leaned a broom or fork against the wall he knocked it down; he tried to climb into the wheelbarrow and almost upset it. Just as Noel was beginning to feel hot and exasperated there was a sound of hoofs and the Radcliffe's appeared. Everything will be O.K. now, she thought, until she saw it was the Radcliffe family minus Hilary and Roger.

"Hallo, Noel," shouted Evelyn. "We've come without Roger and Hilary; they've gone on a scientific expedition."

30

Margaret yelled, "Oh, Noel, you haven't gone and mucked out Harmony? Oh, you are a beast, I wanted to do her."

Evelyn said, "Oh, shut up, Marga, don't make such a fuss."

"I'll muck out Ariel instead," said Margaret, and she dragged Northwind off towards the barn. The other Radcliffe's followed. While they were away, Christopher Minton appeared on a bicycle.

"Hallo, Noel," he called across the yard; "*I'm* in good time, aren't I?"

"Yes, wonderful time," Noel answered, "but the Radcliffes arrived first; they're tying their ponies up."

"Who's left to do?" asked Christopher.

"Only Ariel, and Margaret Radcliffe wants to do him."

"Oh, she can buzz off," said Christopher. "I'm going to do him." He took Noel's pitchfork.

"She'll be furious," said Noel. "Must you, Christopher? She did ask specially."

"I'll deal with Margaret," answered Christopher. "You leave her to me. Have you finished with the wheelbarrow? And have you got a broom?"

"Shan't be a sec," answered Noel, sweeping frantically, "but there are several more brooms by the muck-heap."

"That's all right, I'll wait and have yours."

"Christopher, I bagged to do him," came an angry shout from Margaret. "Noel, why didn't you stop him?"

"I tried to," answered Noel.

"Oh, you are *feeble*," said Margaret angrily, her face scarlet with rage, clashing horribly with the carroty red of her hair. "He knew I wanted to muck out Ariel," she complained to Evelyn.

"Oh, shut up," said Christopher. "If you want to do something you can empty the wheelbarrow for me."

"You can empty your own beastly wheelbarrow. I shall go and groom Doomsday."

"Here's James," called Christopher, "you're doing nothing, empty this wheelbarrow for me."

31

"O.K.," he said, "I'll empty it. Where does it go?"

"Use your eyes," said Christopher.

By the time Ariel's box was done and James had pushed wheelbarrows spilling dirty straw to the muckheap and carried hay and clean straw from the Dutch barn, leaving a trail behind him, the yard looked a shambles. "Oh dear," said Noel, "I suppose we shall have to sweep the whole thing and it'll take hours."

"Leave it," Christopher told her. "I expect Victor will do it while we're out exercising."

"He's busy with the brood mares and anyway Henry said that he was in a mood. I'd better do it."

"I'm going to groom Ariel," said Christopher. Noel began to sweep. Clouds of dust rose up from the yard and with every stroke of the broom it seemed to grow bigger and more untidy. James Radcliffe came to help, but he swept aimlessly and without effect.

"Here I am, late as always," shrieked Susan, clattering into the yard on Golden Wonder. "Oh good, you haven't finished all the work."

"We've done most of it," said Christopher, looking out of Ariel's box. "I've been here since half-past eight."

"I couldn't help it," Susan explained, "Mummy was in one of her awful moods at breakfast."

With Susan helping, the yard soon began to look tidier. The work was getting done somehow: Christopher had finished Ariel and was grooming Apollo. Evelyn had done Harmony and the Widow; Noel had just agreed with Susan that it was quite fun to run the Folly Court stables when there was a terrific crash and Doomsday shot out into the yard.

"Loose horse," yelled Christopher. Susan and Noel dropped their brooms and hurried towards Doomsday; he dodged by them and trotted round the yard. An eager head with hay hanging from its mouth appeared over every loose-box door. Truant began to rear up, threatening to jump out.

Noel shouted to James to shut Truant's top door and

ran for oats. Oh dear, he's sure to get out on the road, she thought. She scooped oats into the bucket and ran back. Susan had a head collar. Doomsday was squealing with Harmony, but directly he saw them advancing he gave a buck, cantered across the yard with his tail looped high over his back and, turning through the gate, he trotted down the drive, snorting in triumph.

"Oh dear," moaned Noel.

Christopher said, "If anyone had had any sense they'd have shut the gate."

"Why *did* you let him out, Marga?" grumbled Susan.

"I couldn't help it. It's not my fault the Major's horses are so nervous. How was I to know he'd be frightened by my vaulting on him from the manger? None of our horses mind."

Susan said, "Honestly, you just don't seem to have any sense at all."

And Evelyn added, "Well, at least you might bolt the door before you begin your trick riding."

Noel was running down the drive, imagining the horrible sight she was going to see when she turned out on the road, when she heard hoofs coming to meet her and the big brown horse appeared again. He was moving at a very slow cadenced trot and wearing a smug expression on his face. Noel held out the bucket of oats, but he trotted by her and then suddenly set off at a gallop. She began to run again. What were the others doing? Why didn't they come and help? she wondered dismally. Out of breath, she dropped into a walk. She could hear excited shrieks behind the barn and as she entered the yard Susan appeared. "It's all right," she said. "We cornered him and he's jumped the railings into the park. He's galloping round and bucking like anything. Evelyn's trying to catch him but it's no use. She'll have to wait till he calms down."

"Here's Henry," said Noel.

"He's missed all the excitement," said Susan.

"I should leave him in the park," Henry told Noel. "Let him exercise himself and bring him in if the flies get too

33

bad. But for heaven's sake don't let that wretch Margaret touch any more of Uncle George's horses."

"I'll do my best," answered Noel, "but I don't seem very good at controlling her."

"Tell her to go home—that you can dispense with her services—if she goes on being a nuisance," suggested Henry. "You must take a firm line with your assistants."

"O.K. I'll take the tack. You'll never catch that bus if you don't go and change."

"Thanks awfully," said Henry, as he began to run.

Noel put Echo's tack away and joined Susan who was sweeping. "I have a feeling in my bones that something awful's going to happen," Noel told her. "You might help me control everyone. It's all very well for Henry to say I should be firm, but no one takes any notice."

"You're always feeling things in your bones," said Susan, "and usually you're wrong. It's only Marga we've got to control—the others are quite sensible—and now she's had a fright she'll probably be all right."

Noel had just caught a glimpse of Henry, looking tall and thin in a suit, running down the drive, when Christopher sauntered up.

"Haven't you two finished *yet*?" he asked. "All the horses are groomed. I suppose I'd better go and catch Doomsday; Evelyn's given up."

"Henry said leave him. It'll save exercising."

"But I want to exercise him," protested Christopher. "I'm not going to be done out of my ride. It won't take *me* long to catch him."

"Can't you ride the Widow?" asked Noel.

"No, Evelyn wants her. and anyway I prefer Doomsday. I'll ride Spartan though, if you like."

"No, you can't," said Noel quickly.

Christopher laughed. "Henry thinks he's the only person who can ride," he said. "You wait till the Major comes home. I bet he lets me ride Spartan."

"Henry doesn't think he's the only person who can

34

ride," Noel spoke angrily. "But he's responsible for all the horses and all the people and—"

"All right, all right. Keep your hair on. I'll go and catch Doomsday." He wandered away in the direction of the park, whistling and swinging a head collar.

"I don't know how you can call *him* sensible," said Noel, trying to master her anger.

"Well, he is in a way," answered Susan. "He's irritating sometimes, but he knows how to do everything and he's a good rider. I expect he *would* manage Spartan."

"I shall be glad when to-day's over," said Noel, beginning to sweep again. "Will you lunge me when we get back from the ride?"

"Yes, O.K.," agreed Susan, "but I've got to go home the minute I've had lunch. I've got to change and drive with Mummy to see Valerie's new home. I can't see why they want me; they'll only talk about chair-covers and curtains all afternoon and I shall be bored stiff. I tried to get out of going, but Mummy said that it was unnatural not to want to see my sister's new house."

"I suppose it is really," said Noel thoughtfully.

"No, it isn't, not if your sister's years older than you and like Valerie."

Christopher appeared riding Doomsday bareback, with a triumphant smile on his face, just as Noel and Susan finished sweeping.

"I've bagged the Italian saddle," he said.

"Beast!" said Evelyn. "I meant to try it."

"You ought to let Evelyn have it," said Margaret. "You had it yesterday."

"You shut up. I'm just about fed up with you."

"Greedy pig, selfish beast," yelled Margaret.

When at last they were ready to start, the sound of hoofs was heard and into the yard rode Philippa and Marion Hunter, one on Crusoe—a bright bay gelding of 15.1—and the other on a bicycle.

"Hallo," said the Folly Court people.

"We hope you don't mind us coming like this," said

35

Philippa nervously. "We wanted some help; we heard that Major Holbrooke's nephew was here and we thought that he might give us advice about Crusoe."

Christopher asked, "What's the trouble? I'll advise you." But Noel spoke up more firmly than usual. "Henry, the Major's nephew, has gone to London to-day," she told them, "but he'll be here to-morrow."

"Oh well, we can come again then," said Philippa in rather disappointed tones. Susan asked, "Why don't you come for a ride with us? We're just going."

The Hunters looked at each other. "We'd love to," said Marion. "It's your turn, Philippa," she added.

"Oh, of course, I forgot you've only Crusoe between you. Here, Marion, you ride Wonder," said Susan dismounting.

"No, no, I couldn't possibly," Marion objected. "It's quite all right—really. It's Philippa's turn and we're quite used to staying behind. I don't mind a bit."

Noel said, "I'd lend you Truant if he wasn't so unreliable."

"Do have Wonder, Marion. Go on, please," pleaded Susan. They argued until Christopher interrupted them. "Are you coming or aren't you, Susan?" he demanded. "You can't expect us to stand here all morning."

They chose a wooded ride; for the fields were baked to a brick-like consistency and the lanes were hot and dusty. Except that Christopher kept Noel on tenterhooks by pointing out what he described as smashing jumps and she was afraid lest she should have to use her authority to stop him jumping them, the ride was very peaceful. Tranquil behaved very well and Susan spent a great deal of time riding beside Noel and admiring him.

Philippa told Christopher all about her troubles with Crusoe and they arranged that Christopher should try jumping him in the school.

Back at Folly Court they found John Manners and Samson waiting in the yard with Marion.

"Here, you take Doomsday," Christopher told Philippa, "I'll go and give Crusoe a canter round."

John said, "Hallo, Noel, I hear Henry's gone to see the Holbrookes; it's a pity. I brought Samson over to see what you two made of him."

"Come and give him a jump, John," shouted Christopher. "I'm going to sharpen Crusoe up for the Hunters."

"For goodness sake' don't smash anything," said Noel.

"I won't," answered Christopher carelessly, "and if I do the Major won't eat me, he and I are good friends. Lawks, do you call this a saddle?"

"Yes," answered Marion, and Philippa asked anxiously, "Is something wrong with it?"

"There's nothing right about it," Christopher answered scornfully. "I'll have the Major's saddle, thank you very much. Get it, Marion, will you?"

"Poor little boy," said Margaret in taunting tones. "He can't ride on that nasty hard saddle."

"Shut up and mind your own business," said Christopher furiously, as he turned and hit out at her with his whip. Margaret dodged out of reach. "Temper, temper," she mocked.

"One of these days I really will deal with you," threatened Christopher.

"This year, next year, some time, never."

Christopher flung his whip.

"Bad luck, missed," said Margaret, and flung it back. It missed Christopher but hit Crusoe. He shot forward in surprise and the Major's saddle, which Marion was putting on, nearly fell to the ground.

"Oh, Margaret, do be careful," said Philippa.

"Now he'll be afraid of whips," said Marion miserably.

"Oh fuss, fuss," said Margaret. "It didn't hurt him."

"You jolly nearly bust up the Major's saddle though," said Christopher through compressed lips. "I shall tell Henry about this to-morrow, I shall tell him to chuck you out. You're nothing but a pest."

"You shouldn't be using the Major's saddle," answered

37

Margaret. "And if you try to stop me coming I shall tell Henry you stretched the saddle putting it on Crusoe."

"Henry will listen to me," said Christopher, riding off.

Susan was lunging Noel on Tranquil. Noel felt disappointed; she didn't seem a bit better than she had been the day before. She was still bouncing about all over the saddle and if for a few moments she did seem to be improving she always found that it was because she had begun to grip with her knees or calves. She had determined to be tough with herself. "Twenty minutes," she told Susan when they began, "and not too much of it at the walk." She regretted her decision many times before the twenty minutes were over.

Christopher told the Hunters to put up some jumps and he began to canter round the outside of the school. Susan took Noel more into the centre. "Crusoe goes much better for Christopher," she said. "He's rather wasted on the Hunters really."

"They've got to learn some time"; Noel sounded disinterested. "I only hope that nothing gets bust."

When the Hunters had built a course to Christopher's liking, Susan said that Noel's twenty minutes were up. "I'll take Tranquil in," said Noel, dismounting thankfully, "and then come back to watch." Her legs felt even worse than they had the day before. I don't believe I shall ever get any better, she thought dismally as she watered Tranquil. I'm doomed to be mediocre. She wandered back to the school feeling hot and exhausted and wishing that it would rain.

Christopher was hitting Crusoe, who had apparently refused the parallel bars, which stood at about three feet three. Christopher turned him round and rode at them again, kicking hard. This time Crusoe jumped though he took off too near. Christopher rode on at the gate. Crusoe looked as though he was going to jump, but at the last moment he refused; he slid into the gate, knocking it down and nearly falling down himself.

"I know he's going to bust something," Noel told John.

38

"Put it up," Christopher told the Hunters. "Come on, you miserable old devil," he said, hitting Crusoe again.

"Poor Crusoe," Noel murmured to John, and then she suggested, "Why don't you bring Samson over to-morrow when Henry's here?"

"Yes, that's the best thing," John had agreed. "I'd better be going now, there's dozens of things to do on the farm."

When John had gone Noel fed the horses and then she climbed the railings into the park and lay under a huge shady oak to eat her sandwiches. I'm being terribly unsociable, she thought, but I can't sit there watching them all admiring Christopher crashing and banging round those jumps. I'm not jealous—at least I don't think so—it's just watching someone doing something all wrong and hearing the silly audience admiring it that's so irritating. Christopher used to be rather nice, she thought, so happy-go-lucky and gay, but now—perhaps I'm just in a bad mood. Her thoughts were interrupted by Susan calling her from the yard.

"Hallo," yelled Noel, "I'm here—in the park." Susan appeared. "Whatever are you doing out there?"

"Having lunch and cooling off," answered Noel.

"The others are all having lunch on top of the new haystack by the barn. It's a super place; Christopher's been up and dug out a hole."

"Sounds hot to me," said Noel. "I prefer the park. But you go on, Susan. I like being alone."

"All right," answered Susan, "if you're sure."

When Noel was revived by solitude and lunch, she wandered back to the yard. Victor was hanging about; he was wearing a tartan shirt, a shiny blue suit, and his hair was heavily smarmed down. He approached Noel at once. It's my 'alf day, to-day. By rights I should 'ave been off at twelve, but I stayed on and saw to the mares. I just want to pop into Gunston, shan't be long, if you can manage this lot all right. I'll see to the mares after I've 'ad my tea."

Noel said, "Oh dear, Henry must have forgotten; but still, we can manage, I suppose; there's quite a few of us."

"I'll be on my way then," said Victor hastily. "I wants to catch the two o'clock bus."

That means the afternoon mucking out, thought Noel. Victor's been doing that. Then there's the tack and we ought to groom the horses again; but I expect if we just brush off their saddle marks it will do. I'd better hurry up with Truant.

As Noel was mounting, the Radcliffes, Susan and Christopher came into the yard. Their hair was full of hay.

"We've had a super fight," Margaret told Noel. Susan said, "Oh, Noel, you should have come up."

"It's Victor's half-day," said Noel, "so we shall have to do the boxes."

"What fun," said Susan. "I do wish I could stay. Bother Valerie's silly house."

"Leave my tack," Christopher told Noel. "I'll clean it to-morrow. I've got to be at the tennis club by three."

"Oh dear, I'm sure leaving dirty tack won't be popular," said Noel drearily.

"Well, James'll clean it for me then."

"Oh no, he jolly well won't. You clean your own beastly tack," answered Margaret quickly.

"I'll do the Widow's," said Evelyn, "but we can't stay long. We've got our ponies to do when we get back."

Noel said, "Oh well, I suppose I shall manage somehow," and she rode out of the yard feeling like someone who is alone on a sinking ship.

When Noel reached the road she tried to stop thinking about her grievances. Truant wasn't going well; he wasn't on the bit; she could detect a stiffness in him somewhere, but her new seat felt perilously insecure and she was incapable of driving him on.

I ought to be enjoying myself, she thought miserably. After all, I might be typing in an office or lying in a nursing home like the Major. It was very hot riding across the unshaded stubble fields and Noel's thoughts were before her, already enjoying the coolness of the breeze which lurked along the ridge. She did not notice the farm implement, shrouded by a tarpaulin, which stood beside the track. Nor did Truant, until he was upon it, then he swung round in terror and galloped, with all the speed he possessed, back down the track.

Noel picked herself up from the prickly stubble. "Truant," she called despairingly after the flying bay form, but the black tail disappeared round a bend and he was lost to view. She felt like sitting down and bursting into tears. There were all those stables to muck out, seven dirty horses to groom, the tack to clean, and now she must spend hours catching Truant even if he didn't gallop straight out on the road and crash into a lorry. For the second time that day, she set off in pursuit. She ran down the hot, dusty track until she could run no more; when she regained her breath, she ran again. At length she came to the Brampton road; there was no sign of Truant and no one to tell her which way he had gone. She took the way which led to Folly Court. He'd probably go back to Tranquil, she thought, and if he doesn't meet a car he'll probably fall down as he turns up the drive and break both his knees.

But round the next bend a glad sight met her eyes. A small dark girl on a grey pony was leading a sweating Truant. Noel recognised Gay Millwood.

"Is he yours?" shouted Gay. Noel answered, "Yes. I fell off. Where did you catch him?"

"Just up the road. He came trotting along. I think he was pleased to be caught; he looked very miserable, but he saw that Biddy was a motherly sort of pony."

"Poor Truant," said Noel, looking him over for injuries but finding none; even the reins were unbroken. "It was terribly nice of you to catch him," she told Gay, "but for you I'm sure that he would have been run over or broken his knees; thank you very much."

"That's quite all right," answered Gay. "I knew some-one must have fallen off, but I didn't recognise him; have you had him long?"

"No," said Noel, mounting. "Only this summer. I've got two. I'm supposed to be breaking them in."

41

"He's lovely," said Gay, riding beside Noel.

Noel looked at her watch. "Oh dear," she said, "I must hurry. I shall never get those stables done."

"How many horses have you got altogether then?" asked Gay.

"Oh, they're not mine, they're the Major's," Noel said, and she began to explain the situation at Folly Court. By the time she had finished explaining they had reached the Court and, at the gate, Gay said: "I'll come and help you. I expect I can be of some use."

"That's nice of you," said Noel. "But what about your parents? Won't they fuss if you don't turn up to tea?"

"No, they're used to me. Mummy's given up worrying."

Noel had expected to find the yard deserted; she was very surprised when she saw a figure sitting outside the saddle room and realised that it was Dick Hayward.

"Hallo, what are you doing here?" she asked.

"Hallo, Noel," said Dick. "I might have asked the same of you, but I met John and he told me about everything. I came along to offer my services."

Noel said, "That's awfully nice of you. Gay's going to help too so we shall get everything done very speedily."

It didn't take them long to do the boxes. Noel and Dick mucked out, straightened the beds and filled the water buckets, Gay rushed backwards and forwards with the wheelbarrow. They brushed over all the horses and rugged up those that wore rugs. Dick carried a whole bale of hay round from the barn to save spilling it all over the yard. Noel mixed the feeds.

It was evening by the time they had cleaned the tack; the sun was low and the sky a faded blue. A sound of contented munching came from the stables.

Noel said, "It's wonderfully cool."

"Just as well; I've got a bicycle home."

Gay was mounting Biddy. "Good-bye," she said, "thanks tons for letting me help."

"Thank *you* for helping and for catching Truant," said Noel, "you've been terribly useful."

"Would it be all right if I came to-morrow?"

"Yes, of course. We'd love to have you."

Dick said, "I'll be up too, Noel. I don't quite know what time. I shall come over on Crispin."

Dick helped Noel to saddle Truant and brought out Tranquil when she was mounted.

"Good night," he said.

"Good night," Noel answered, "and thanks awfully. I can't think what I would have done without you."

After dinner Noel telephoned Folly Court. Henry was back, and Noel told him all that had happened, but he had hardly begun to relate his adventures when Professor Kettering appeared and asked for how much longer did Noel intend to monopolise the telephone as he had an important call to make?

Noel told Henry, and he said that all his news could wait till the morrow, so she rang off. She was most indignant afterwards when she found that her father's call wasn't important at all and that he was merely gossiping with a fellow archaeologist about fishing.

CHAPTER FOUR

NOEL arrived at Folly Court at five minutes to eight on Friday morning expecting to find Henry just beginning work, but she knew by the state of the yard that a good deal of mucking out had already been done.

Henry's head appeared over Ariel's door. "Good morning," he said. "Here, I want to ask you something."

"When I came out this morning there was no Victor," he told her, "but mucking out Doomsday was a small dark female whom, to the best of my belief, I have never seen before. She told me that she had given all the horses some hay but no oats as she didn't know how many they were supposed to have. She's tremendously competent and I've had to hurry like mad to keep up with her; at intervals there's a shout of 'wheelbarrow' and it's dumped outside the door. Who is she?"

"It sounds like Gay Millwood; you know, I told you about her catching Truant when I fell off yesterday."

"Yes, but this person only looks about nine."

"That'll be Gay. She does look about nine though I think she's eleven. She said she was coming to help, but I didn't think she'd be here as early as this."

"She's been here hours," said Henry. "Heaven knows at what dreadful moment she rose."

Noel found Gay mucking out Harmony. "Hallo," she said, "you've horrified Henry by your early rising."

"I got up at six. It was *super*. I'm choosing the best-behaved-looking horses to muck out. I hope that's all right?"

At eight-thirty, when Victor turned up, looking more shifty-eyed than ever, and explained to Henry that he had overslept, all the boxes were mucked out; there remained only the yard to be swept.

Henry said, "Well, you'd better groom a couple of

horses for us and then go up to the mares. I saw my uncle yesterday," he went on. "He says that Ariel and Apollo are to abandon their education until things are better organised. We're to keep Spartan, Doomsday and the Widow up because he hopes to be able to hunt them; but Harmony's to have her shoes off because he definitely won't be fit for any dressage tests this summer."

"That'll be an 'elp," Victor said grudgingly. "Course we 'aven't been able to see to things properly like, since the Major's accident; not with all them 'orses in, and Fred and Blake going sick—that topped the lot."

"That's right," answered Henry, "and my uncle hopes to be home in a fortnight and he's going to see about getting some more staff."

When Victor had gone to groom Spartan, Noel asked, "Did you tell the Major that Blake was in bed?"

Henry grinned. "Not exactly," he said. "I was very diplomatic. I told him all about Blake being kicked, but I said that he couldn't do *much*. I didn't actually say so, but I led my poor uncle to believe that Blake spends his time hobbling round the yard giving us advice."

"Do you think they will be home in a fortnight?"

"Uncle George seemed to think so; he was fairly definite about it. Aunt Carol will be out of plaster by then, which means that one of them will have two hands. They were both tremendously cheerful and Uncle G. has resigned himself to finding his horses unschooled."

"Lawkes! What a difference it makes having Henry in charge," said Christopher, bicycling into the yard. "You should have seen it yesterday when Noel was boss—talk about a pigsty! How's the Major?" he went on. "Is he going to be home to train us for the inter-branch?"

"No," Henry answered. "He's not coming home for a fortnight and when he does he's taking life quietly and not wearing himself out for the Pony Club."

"Oh well, I shall drop dressage for the summer then. I'm fed up with schooling and there's no point in going on if one isn't going to get any encouragement."

"What amazing opinions these young people do express. We've never had anything but discouragement, have we, Noel? Yet we plod on in the face of fearsome odds."

Christopher looked hurt and Noel said hastily, "I was terribly discouraged yesterday. Lunging doesn't seem to be making much difference to me, but I suppose one must go on. After all, at the Spanish School of Vienna they lunge one every day for three months."

"A silly fad, I should think. Except, of course, that some people do have naturally better seats than others."

"I'll go and see Blake now," Henry said, as he swept the last heap into Gay's shovel. "It's nine o'clock; he ought to be visible and I can't see any point in keeping Ariel and Apollo in a moment longer than we need. Uncle George said, tell Blake to turn them out and I didn't like to ask where, for fear of arousing his suspicions."

"I'll groom Echo for you," offered Christopher.

Noel said, "That leaves the Widow and Harmony."

The next Pony Club member to arrive was Dick. He was most indignant to find that all the work was done.

When the last horse was groomed they sat down on the plot of grass in the middle of the yard, to wait for Henry.

"This is lovely," said Noel, chewing a blade of grass.

"We ought to be riding before it gets hot and before that silly little fool Margaret arrives. *Why* doesn't Henry get a move on?" Christopher complained.

Noel said, "I'm enjoying this. I've done nothing but hurry for three days. I like life to be peaceful."

"Oh, Noel, you do sound ancient," said Gay.

Just as Christopher, bored with waiting, had collected several little heaps of straw and dried grass and was igniting them with his cigarette lighter, Henry appeared. "We've settled everything," he said. "Ariel and Apollo are to go out with the two-year-olds and Harmony with the brood mares. I'm going to ring up Hodges now, about having her shoes off."

"I'll turn out Ariel and Apollo," said Christopher, getting up and stamping out his tiny fires.

46

"O.K., but get Dick or Noel to lead one of them."
Henry ran off in the direction of the house and the other
four fetched head collars for Ariel and Apollo.

"What *does* the Major do with so many?" asked Gay,
when she saw the two-year-olds and the yearlings in their
big paddocks and the mares with foals standing in their
loose-boxes. "He sells quite a few," answered Noel, "but
he's always lamenting the fact that so few people know
how to break and school them."

"I wish he'd give me one," said Christopher, as they
watched Ariel and Apollo galloping round. "I'd ride it in
adult jumping competitions and dressage tests. William's
a grand old pony, but he's getting on in years and won't
last me for ever. I shall have to hand him down to David
and Martin. They'll never ride him properly—but still."

Christopher was annoyed when they returned to the
yard and found it full of horses and ponies.

"There," he said, "I knew that would happen: now we
shall have that blasted Margaret interfering."

The Radcliffes were there, except for Roger. Susan had
come and John and the Hunters. Henry joined Noel.
"Hodges is coming at two o'clock," he said, and then, in a
lower voice, he added, "I don't want to take this rabble
out for a ride. We'd better lunge and school and perhaps
there will be a few less by this afternoon. We might ask
Hilary and John to lunge us, then we could both be done
at once."

Hilary and John were delighted to lunge, but instead of
the others taking themselves off for a hack as Henry had
hoped, they all came to watch.

"I think *we* ought to be lunged," Philippa said loudly to
Marion. "If it improves good riders like Henry and Noel
it would be sure to improve us."

"It doesn't, that's just the point," said Evelyn. "It
hasn't done them a bit of good so far."

"Here, give it a fair trial," objected Dick. "Noel's been
lunged three times and I believe I'm right in saying that
this is only Henry's second attempt."

47

"I'll try it to-day," said Christopher, "just to see if there's anything in it."

"I shall ask Henry to lunge me," said Philippa.

And Marion said, "Oh, Philippa, you *can't*."

Philippa said no more, but directly Henry dismounted, she hurried across the school to ask him.

Henry gave a little bow, "Delighted," he said, much to Marion's surprise. Philippa mounted Echo and Henry took the lunge rein from John.

"Hoy, Henry. You can't do that," Christopher shouted. "I wanted you to lunge me."

"Hurrah! Another convert," replied Henry. "Ask Noel if you can have Tranquil, or queue." Christopher looked cross. "Do you want a go, John?" asked Noel as she dismounted. John looked embarrassed; he muttered something about it not being quite his cup of tea.

Susan said, "Oh, Noel, lunge me, *please*. I want to know what it feels like."

"All right. You can have Tranquil. But you're not to shriek. I don't want his nerves upset."

"O.K., I promise," said Susan. "Ooh, it does feel queer," she said, as Tranquil walked round.

Though Susan fooled about, giggled and made no effort at all to sit properly Noel soon realised, to her chagrin, that Susan's seat was much better than either Henry's or her own. She doesn't really drop her knees low enough, thought Noel, examining Susan critically, but she sits on the right part of herself. That's how she's done so well and managed to get into the Pony Club team, I suppose, because she doesn't take riding seriously; she never schools or tries to improve.

Henry didn't lunge Philippa for long. She puffed and gasped and bounced about so much that he began to think that she would collapse from exhaustion. At the end of ten minutes he said, "There, I think that's enough for your first go. Christopher," he shouted when Philippa had thanked him, "your turn."

"Do you want to go on?" Noel asked Susan. "Not parti-

48

cularly," Susan answered. "It's quite fun at first, but it soon gets monotonous. Goodness," she went on, testing both her legs carefully, "I don't ache a bit."

"Oh, you are *lucky*," groaned Philippa, "I ache all over."

"I can't have been working," said Susan.

"No, it's not that," Noel told her, "it's just that you already have a better seat than most of us."

Susan looked pleased. "Go on," she said, "you'll be telling me I'm good enough for Wembley next."

"Do you want a go, Marion?" asked Noel.

"Oh yes, *please*."

Marion was just as bad as Philippa. She hung on to the pommel grimly; soon her face was scarlet with the effort of trying to remain in the correct position. Noel told Tranquil to walk. "You're much too stiff," she said to Marion, "I think if you tried a bit less hard you might get on better."

Henry found Christopher irritating to lunge. It was at once apparent to him that Christopher sat better than he did himself and it was obvious from Christopher's behaviour that he had realised this too. He didn't hold on at all. "Of course the great thing is to sit down properly," he said, "and to be supple. The Major was very keen on suppling exercises last summer."

He began to do exercises at the trot. "Give us a canter," he said. "I bet I can touch my toes at the canter."

"He really *is* good, isn't he?" said Philippa in admiring tones. "Oh yes," Susan agreed. "He must be one of the best riders in *all* the Pony Clubs."

When the lunging was over, John asked Henry if he would give him some advice about Samson's jumping. Henry answered that his advice wasn't worth having, but he would gladly give it. Christopher announced that he was going to school Crusoe and would give him a jump or two. The Radcliffes asked if they could jump and Henry said that he supposed so, but that if anyone broke any jumps they would have to replace or repair them. He refused to let Christopher have the show jumps which he had used the day before. He insisted that they should use already battered fences, or poles.

Christopher grumbled. He said that he hadn't broken anything the day before, that he could understand Henry not wanting the whole Pony Club over them, but that he didn't see why he shouldn't jump them—he would square the Major if he *did* break anything.

Henry answered, "Them as don't like the jumps provided can go home and jump their own."

John bestirred Samson into a canter and, kicking hard, rode at the first fence—a pair of elderly wattles. Samson was swerving the whole way up and John was using his reins and legs to keep him straight. Samson refused, John kicked even harder and they lurched over. "There, you see," he said in despairing tones, "that's what always happens."

"Have you tried jumping very low?" asked Henry.

"Yes, poles on the ground and everything."

"Let me have a go," said Christopher. "I should think he just wants sharpening up."

John said, "O.K.," in reluctant tones. Christopher gave Crusoe to Philippa and, mounting Samson, took a very firm feel on his mouth. He kicked and hit him; bustled him into a canter, hauled him round on a circle and then rode at the wattles. Samson refused dead and Christopher went on, over his head. He jumped up quickly and remounted; he was red in the face. He began to hit and kick Samson again.

Noel said, "Do stop him, Henry. We had this for ages yesterday with Crusoe; it doesn't do a bit of good."

"What ought John to do?" Henry asked.

"I don't know. But I don't think it's Samson's jumping that's wrong, I think it's his schooling."

Christopher managed to force Samson over the wattles, but in no better style than he had jumped with John.

"It's no good going on like that," Henry told him. "Forcing him over won't improve matters; we must bring
50

our united intelligences to bear on the matter and try to work out what has gone wrong."

"If I were you, John," said Christopher as he dismounted, "I should ride him in spurs and a double bridle and try to push him together a bit."

John thought for a moment. Then he said, "But one isn't supposed to use a double bridle until the horse goes well in a snaffle."

"Yes, well that's all very well with some horses, but a big sloppy animal like this needs driving together."

"Perhaps you're right," said John doubtfully.

"No, he isn't," said Noel. And Henry said, "Don't abandon your principles too easily, John."

"Is he going to jump?" asked Noel, looking at Christopher. "Because if he is, I'm off. I hate watching all this banging and crashing about."

"I do wish Uncle George was here," said Henry. "I'm sure no other nephew has ever wished for his uncle as often as I. But, truthfully, John, I don't know what to advise, except lots of low jumps and aim to get him going over them freely and as though he was enjoying himself. Noel says that it's his schooling on the flat that's wrong," Henry continued. "She'll recommend you to be lunged."

"I don't mind being lunged if you really think it would improve matters," John said, looking at Noel.

"I don't think anything will improve any of us; we're doomed to failure," said Noel drearily. "Look at that," she went on, drawing their attention to Christopher.

"He goes much better for Christopher than he does for the Hunters," said Susan.

"May I be preserved from seeing the Hunters ride him then," said Noel disagreeably.

John asked, "What's wrong?"

"I wouldn't mind the horse being behind the bit with his hocks trailing out behind him if Christopher didn't look so pleased with himself," said Noel. "He thinks he's collected just because he's pulled the horse's nose in."

Henry said to her, "Come on. We'll feed the horses and

51

then I'll give you a nice long lemonade and you can cool off before lunch."

The week-end passed very peacefully. Everyone except Noel and Henry had entered for the Brampton and district show which was held on Saturday. Noel and Henry wouldn't go despite the encouragement of the other Pony Club members. Noel said how could she enter Truant or Tranquil for anything? They were much too unschooled. And Henry said that he knew only too well how Echo would behave in the showing class and that he was going to stay at home and be lunged. He and Noel lunged each other twice on Saturday, in the morning and again in the afternoon, for they had both decided that it was impossible for them to school their horses with their new seats.

Victor took Sunday afternoon off, and Noel and Henry were still on their own for the other Pony Club members, exhausted by their efforts at the show, were lying in their gardens languidly doing nothing; but with only four horses stabled Noel and Henry managed quite easily even with the extra task of turning out the mares and foals.

Monday began with a thunderstorm. All morning it thundered and lightened and the rain came down in torrents and lay in lakes on the hard, unyielding fields. Noel cleaned her tack, which had been neglected over the week-end and Henry said that he would be virtuous and help her by cleaning the metal parts.

In the afternoon the sun shone on the thirst-quenched woods and fields and they rode along the glistening tracks; first on Echo and Truant and later leading Spartan and Tranquil from Doomsday and the Merry Widow.

On Tuesday everyone appeared again. They converged on Folly Court from all directions and the yard was noisy with discussion of the show.

"Of course you and Noel were quite crazy not to go," Christopher told Henry. "I'm absolutely certain that Echo would have won something in the Riding Horse class, and probably Tranquil too. Crusoe was third and you should have *seen* the show he gave: Philippa made a hopeless muck of it."

"We had a nice, peaceful day 'far from the madding crowd' and all the rest of it," answered Henry. "How many classes did you win?"

"Me? Oh, I had a rather good day. First in the Handy Hunter, the Bending and the Musical Poles, and second in the Potato Race. The only class we didn't get anything in was the Juvenile Jumping, but there was a pretty high standard, and of course William isn't a show jumper. We had four faults."

Noel asked Evelyn how the Radcliffes had fared. "Not too well," Evelyn answered. "Only one first, that was me and Pilot in the Potato Race. I simply had to beat Christopher. I thought he'd be more unbearable than ever if he won all three of the gymkhana events. Hilary was second in the Handy Hunter and she and Marga were third and reserve in the Musical Poles. The Grade C jumping was a bit much," she went on. "The jumps were all the biggest four feet you ever saw, but at least our horses did better than Crusoe and Christopher. They refused three times at the stile."

"Christopher's an idiot to ride him in a Grade C," Noel spoke hotly, "anyone can see he's not ready."

"I heard he'd won them with his last owner."

"Yes, I've heard that too, but at the moment he's afraid of jumping three feet so it's pointless to ride him in a class with jumps of four feet."

"Oh well, I suppose Christopher thought he'd get him round and, after all, there wouldn't be many entries if we all stayed at home like you and Henry, waiting until we were perfect."

Susan interrupted hastily, "Noel, I was hopeless," she said. "You'd better give up copying my seat for it doesn't seem much use. Wonder won the showing, in spite of me, but that was the only class in which we did anything. And

53

you should have seen my circles! Eggs weren't in it, they were more like squashed tomatoes. I *was* thankful the Major wasn't there."

"I'm glad you won," said Noel, "but how did you get on with the jumping?"

"We hit the gate," answered Susan. "But I must say it did look enormous."

John hadn't taken Samson to the show. He had ridden Turpin, for whom he was much too big and heavy, and had won a couple of thirds. He was more depressed than ever and he asked in the dreariest tones if he might be lunged. Philippa and Marion both wanted to be lunged again and Gay asked if anyone could bear to lunge her.

Evelyn said she'd never seen so many mad people and that insanity must be catching, but Hilary said that only rabies was catching and this was mass hysteria.

Christopher had appointed himself chief lunger and he was a hard taskmaster; he had no hesitation in telling the victim his faults. "You're looking at the ground," he told Noel ceaselessly, and he nagged at Philippa and Marion until they stopped holding on.

When the lunging was over Christopher wanted another jumping contest, but Henry hastily arranged a hack, and in the end only Christopher remained behind to school Crusoe and the two Hunters to watch him.

It was on Wednesday that Noel realised that she was improving. She was cantering round on Tranquil when she became aware that she was sitting down quite loosely and without any effort at all. She found herself looking round at the other people, at the trees and the deep dark blue of the sky. She felt very happy, but she said nothing to Christopher. This was only the beginning.

Henry also seemed pleased with himself and as they cleaned tack they and the other people who were being lunged discussed the surprise the Major would have when he came home and found them all riding with wonderful dressage seats. "Only one week more, though," said Henry.

"Noel and I survived two goes a day over the week-end: I suppose no one else would like to try that, just to step the improvement up a bit?"

"I'm all for it," answered Noel.

But the Hunters gave shrieks of horror and John replied with a very emphatic "No."

Henry grinned. "We'll have a private evening session."

"Not to-night," answered Noel, "because we've just cleaned all the tack."

On Thursday Dick, Noel and Henry mucked out. Victor seemed to have abandoned the stabled horses altogether; he devoted all his time to the mares and foals.

"Perhaps he can't face working with us," said Noel. "Our lack of method must be maddening."

"If you ask me, he's become bone idle," answered Henry, "but he seems to be looking after the mares all right. I went up last night on a tour of inspection. Anyway, Blake says that he'll be about again on Monday which will authenticate my white lies before the return of my esteemed uncle and aunt."

"We shall have to do some tidying up before they return," said Noel. "The yard isn't bad, but it hasn't that speckless appearance one associates with Folly Court."

"What about the school?" said Henry. "That's going to take hours to restore, and Christopher has got to do his share, because he's made most of the mess."

The mucking out and grooming was done so briskly and efficiently that Dick was lunging Henry before any of the other Pony Club members had arrived. Noel, waiting her turn with Tranquil, was able to watch.

"You have improved," she told Henry after a few minutes. "You look *miles* better. Much more like a proper dressage person."

Everyone else arrived at once and there was the usual clamour to be lunged. Henry said he would lunge Noel and Christopher bagged the other lunge rein for Philippa and Crusoe. Then John explained that he was in a hurry; they were expecting the combine harvester to arrive that morning and make a start on the wheat. "I'll improvise," offered Hilary. She returned in a few moments carrying a pair of driving reins and a hunting whip. "I always improvised in the days of the horsebreakers," she said. "I can't stand people who won't do anything without all the right bits and pieces."

Three people being lunged at once made rather a squash in the school, but with a little organisation it could be managed. The victims were just beginning to puff and blow and demand a rest at the walk, when the sound of a car was heard; no one took any notice until a few minutes later when a well-known voice inquired, "What's going on here?" And Major Holbrooke. with one arm in plaster, appeared at the gate.

"Lawkes!" said Christopher.

Henry said, "Uncle George! What the devil are you doing *here*? You told me a fortnight. The reception committee is quite unprepared; we haven't even put 'welcome home' over the front door."

"I thought I'd save you the trouble," answered the Major. "But what *is* going on here? Are they in training for the Olympics?"

"Yes. We've all been working very hard in your absence, and you can avert your eyes from the school because we're going to rake it this afternoon. Here, Dick, will you take Noel? Shall we go on a tour of inspection?" he asked the Major, "or ought you to be in bed?"

"Good heavens, no! I'm perfectly all right now, except for this confounded arm. Where's Blake? When I came through the yard there wasn't a soul to be seen."

"He's up at his cottage," said Henry, trying not to look guilty. "His knee's giving him a lot of trouble."

"Oh dear," said Noel as Henry and the Major walked down the path to the yard. "Poor Henry; his tangled web has caught up with him. Let's stop, Dick. I haven't the strength after the shock of the Major's sudden appearance. Besides, we ought to start raking the school."

56

"I don't know what you're making this fuss about," said Dick calmly. "You've been looking after the Major's horses all this time and now you behave as though you were trespassing or something."

"That's what I feel like," answered Noel.

"And if we tidy up the school and melt away who's going to muck out and exercise to-morrow?" asked Dick. "Henry's got to do the lot, I suppose, or is the Major going to help him with his arm in plaster?"

"He's getting another groom; he told Henry so."

"I suppose if he advertises to-day he'll have one ready to start work by to-morrow," said Dick sarcastically. "You said you wanted to be lunged for half an hour and you've only had twenty minutes, including nattering. If you want to stop now you'll have to jump for it."

"Beast!" said Noel.

"I'll start tidying up," offered Marion, and she began to collect the jumps and put them back in their original pile. "I'll go and look for rakes," said Susan.

Philippa, gasping for breath, said, "Please, please, Christopher, mayn't I walk: just for a minute?" And when she had regained her breath, she went on, "I do wish the Major hadn't come back, because it means you won't be able to jump and school Crusoe for us any more."

"Not necessarily," answered Christopher. "I'm on pretty good terms with the Major. I expect he'll let me go on jumping, and if he won't, I'll have to come over to your place, that's all."

"Yes, but we haven't any jumps," said Philippa.

"Well, you can get some," Christopher told her.

"Marion," shouted Hilary. "Your turn. John says you can have Samson if you buck up."

"Oh, thank you, John," answered Marion as she approached, "but hadn't I better tidy up? We don't want to annoy Major Holbrooke."

John said, "I'll get on with the clearing up for a quarter of an hour, while you have Samson, and then I must be off, because of the combine."

Noel's half-hour ended as Susan and Gay returned laden with rakes and hoes.

"I'm just going to put Tranquil away," Noel told them, "then I'll come and help." But in the yard she met the Major and Henry.

"This is Tranquil, is it?" said the Major, standing back and studying him. "They're two nice horses, Noel," he said at length, "I shall be interested to see how they go."

"They're both terribly green," said Noel drearily, and she hurried Tranquil into his loose-box.

"We've rather abandoned our schooling," Henry told the Major. "We decided to concentrate on ourselves we thought it might prove the best policy in the end."

"Very likely," said the Major in non-committal tones. "Well, I shall go in now and see what your aunt is up to. She's probably fussing round her birds and wearing herself out when she ought to be resting."

"I'll come in when I've had a word with Noel," said Henry. He leaned over Tranquil's door. Noel was unsaddling. "Does he mind?" she asked.

"Mind? What?" Henry inquired.

"About us and the mess and Blake and everything."

"Oh no, I don't think so. He's resigned to the mess and us. I buzzed off while he was talking to Blake so I don't know what Blake told him. It's no use worrying; we've held the fort and done no irretrievable damage. I'll just go and see Aunt Carol and then I'll come back and discuss plans for this afternoon."

"I shall be in the school. We're going to rake it."

She watered Tranquil, thinking that everything was over now and she hadn't realised before how much she was enjoying herself. I'm terribly glad the Major's better, she thought, but he won't want us all over the place borrowing his school, his lunge whips and reins. I suppose Henry can ride over to Russet Cottage and we can lunge in Farmer Cox's field, but probably he'll want to stay here and get some advice from the Major.

Everyone had stopped work in the school; they were

standing in a group all looking down at someone in their midst. "What's happened?" asked Noel.

"It's Marga; she's knocked out."

"That ass Christopher hit her with a rake."

"*She's* all right; I didn't hit her a bit hard."

"What about a glass of water?"

"Oughtn't we to telephone for a doctor?"

"Oh, Christopher," said Noel, "just as the Holbrookes get home."

"It was her fault," Christopher defended himself. "She turned the hose on me; look, I'm completely *soaked*."

"For goodness' sake all get back a bit and give her some air," said Hilary.

"I'll go and ring up Doc," said Evelyn. But at that moment Margaret sat up. "I'm all right," she said.

"You're going to have a beautiful black eye," said Dick.

"Have you got a headache?" asked Hilary.

"No, of course not," she climbed to her feet.

Christopher said, "It was your own silly fault."

"Oh shut up," Evelyn turned on him. "Whatever she did was no excuse for you to hit her with a rake."

"What do you expect me to do? Just stand and be soaked, I suppose?" demanded Christopher indignantly.

"Well, you're always picking quarrels with her; why can't you leave her alone?"

"She doesn't leave me alone," said Christopher.

"Marga, you'd better come and sit down in the saddle room," Hilary told her.

As Hilary and Evelyn led Margaret away they met Henry returning.

"What's happened now?" he inquired.

"Some people can't keep their tempers," said Evelyn.

Hilary asked, "Could you ring our mother and ask her to collect Marga? She's not fit to ride home."

"I'm all right," said Margaret, pulling away from her sisters. "Do leave me alone."

Henry said, "if you think it's necessary. How did it happen?"

The Radcliffes immediately assumed expressions of determined silence, so Henry turned to Noel.

"Apparently Christopher hit her with a rake," said Noel. "I wasn't here."

"He really is the limit," Henry spoke crossly. "I'll give him a piece of my mind." He turned towards the school.

"Apparently Margaret turned the hose on him," Noel told Henry, "so I dare say she deserved all she got."

"Bashing people over the head with rakes isn't a suitable retaliation for anything," said Henry loudly.

Christopher turned round; he wore a defiant grin. "I thought it was time she was taught a lesson."

"Surely you can control people five years younger than you without half murdering them," said Henry. "You can't just lose your temper and go round knocking people out because they play practical jokes on you."

"It was beyond a joke. Look at me; I'm soaked."

"I remember an occasion when you threw a bucket of water over June Cresswell," said Henry, "and we all thought it a joke, except for her mother."

"That was different," answered Christopher going red in the face; "we were having a water fight."

Henry said, "I'm not one to stand about splitting hairs, but you are requested to remember that my aunt and uncle are only just returned from a nursing home and require peace and quiet." Then he turned to Noel. "It's a bit early, but if we fed the horses now we could take them out directly after lunch."

"I'm going to take both mine home and then bring Truant back this afternoon."

"I'd forgotten about your lunch," Henry told her. "Yes, I suppose it would be more tactful if you didn't stay. I'll come and help you off with your two."

"Henry," shouted Christopher. "Is it all right if I ride Doomsday and Dick the Widow this afternoon?"

60

"Oh, I suppose so," said Henry unwillingly, "that is, if Susan and the Radcliffes don't want to ride."

"Are the birds all right?" asked the Major, as he sat down to lunch.

"Yes, they're fine," answered Mrs. Holbrooke. "I think Archie's missed me a bit, but the others are blooming in the most heartless fashion. How are the horses?"

"They *look* all right, which is surprising enough. Henry didn't give us a true picture of the chaotic conditions. Fred's been away nearly a fortnight, Blake's been in bed over a week, and Victor, well, he never was much good and he made no attempt to rise to the occasion."

"Oh, Henry. But who's done all the work then?"

"The Pony Club, so far as I can make out. They seem to be in possession. The school looked like the Olympic team in training—dozens of people being lunged—the barn is full of ponies and the saddle room of satchels."

"But Henry, you never said a word about this."

Henry, who had been chasing peas round his plate, looked his aunt in the face and answered cheerfully, "How on earth could I? You know as well as I do that Uncle George would have shot straight out of his sick-bed and come tearing home. I *did* tell you about Fred's appendix and that Sportain had kicked Blake. Besides, we managed quite well. Noel was my prop and stay and some of the others were very useful. Since we turned the three greys out we've had a very easy time; we've spent practically all day lunging each other."

"Whose idea was that?" asked the Major.

"Noel's. She and I began and there have been a number of converts."

"Well," said the Major, "those who wish can go on using the school until the end of the holidays. I don't want it and there's no point in letting it lie there idle. And I'll leave you in charge of the horses for another week. I've advertised for some more staff, but I shan't hear anything before Monday."

CHAPTER FIVE

WHEN Henry told the Pony Club members that the Major said they were to be in charge for another week and might go on using the school until the end of the holidays, they were all delighted.

"I was afraid that the Holbrookes coming back would spoil all the fun," said Susan, "but now we can go on just as we were before."

Noel said, "It's nice of him to lend us the school."

"I'm going to ask if I can go on exercising the horses when he's got the new groom," Christopher announced. "I should think he'd be quite glad to have me, won't he, Henry? Grooms aren't normally much good at riding."

"I haven't an idea," answered Henry shortly.

But though they all turned up with their lunches and mucked out and groomed, exercised and were lunged, it wasn't quite as it had been before. The Holbrookes' presence made everyone a little less carefree and much less noisy. Only Henry, relieved of the greater part of his responsibility, was more cheerful than before.

The Major, having no occupation, strolled about with all the dogs at his heels. They were determined not to lose sight of their master again and they followed him on his restless wanderings round the park and his frequent visits to the school.

Noel hated the Major watching while she was lunged, it put her off altogether, but Christopher said that he didn't care how many people watched him and quarrelled with Henry, who refused to let him jump Crusoe on the grounds that it would give the Major a heart-attack.

Blake began to hobble down to the yard leaning heavily on a stick. He was horrified by the untidiness of the saddle room and the baling wire that was scattered all over the hay barn, but he seemed satisfied with the appearance of the horses. He and the Major spent a lot of time sitting in the sun and poring over letters from prospective second men and experienced girl grooms.

The Holbrookes had been home exactly a week when the Major said suddenly at lunch, "I think I shall run a course for these children; they're much keener than I thought, if the industry in the school is any indication."

"George, don't be silly," said Mrs. Holbrooke bluntly. "Even when you've been in the best of health, thoses courses have always exhausted you."

"In the past I've always had a great many other things to do at the same time. It was trying to fit everything in, not the course itself, that was tiring," answered the Major calmly. "Anyway, it's the lesser of two evils, Carol, because I can't stand this inactivity any longer. The alternative is getting up one of the more sober hunt horses and going out on hound exercise."

"That's out of the question," said Mrs. Holbrooke firmly. "I forbid it and I shall send for Doctor Hastings if you so much as look at any of the hunt horses."

"Do you think the Pony Club would like a course, Henry?" asked the Major, for so far Henry had worn an expressionless face.

"There's no doubt about that. I've never heard so many people wish for one as I've heard these holidays, but we don't want it at the expense of my dear uncle's health. We should all be haunted by remorse for ever if you collapsed with secondary concussion just because of our irritating hopelessness."

"That's settled then," said the Major in very final tones. "You can be secretary of the course, Henry, that'll save me a lot of work. You'd better ask Noel to come to tea this afternoon and we'll discuss whom to invite."

Henry looked at his aunt, but she only made a sign of helpless resignation with her hands.

Henry was very cheerful all that afternoon. But when

63

the Pony Club members asked why he was so pleased with himself he replied mysteriously. He told Noel that the Major had asked her to tea, but he wouldn't tell why. Noel became very apprehensive. She could only imagine unpleasant reasons for the invitation.

"Is he going to give up the Pony Club?" she asked. "Has he decided that he can't have Sonnet turned out with his brood mares after all?"

Henry didn't tell her about the course until the last of the other Pony Club members had ridden away. Noel was less enthusiastic than he had expected.

"Don't you want one?" he asked.

"Yes, I do really, and it's terribly kind of the Major. It's just that Truant and Tranquil are so badly schooled and my seat's in such a muddle. I shall be so hopeless, much worse than everyone else."

Henry grinned. "It's a course," he said, "not a competition. You only want to shine."

"Beast," said Noel. "It isn't that at all. The point is that Tranquil and Truant haven't even reached Sonnet's standard of schooling yet, so what's the use of trying to learn any more?"

"Perhaps Uncle G. won't try to teach us any more. He's got eyes; he must have seen how hopeless we are. Personally I think we ought to go right back to the beginning and go all through it again. It would be like reading a book a second time—you always find masses that you've missed. Shall I suggest it to him?"

"Christopher won't be pleased."

"I don't care about him."

The Major waited until everyone had drunk at least one cup of tea and eaten several egg and cress sandwiches before he began to talk about the course.

"I've been thinking the matter over and I've come to the conclusion that this would be the wrong moment to run a dressage course. I've seen a lot of good work going on in the school and there's no doubt that you're all improving your seats, but the improvement isn't cemented yet and if I ask you to use your seats and backs to drive the horse at this stage, you will either become stiff or relapse into your old bad habits. Then there is the tremendous difference in the education and ability of the horses; we have the old ponies, mostly schooled to the limits of their capabilities, and the young horses, most of them far behind the ponies in their education, but showing greater promise. I could see no way of training these two groups together, without boring the owners of ponies or hurrying the young horses, until I thought of a cross-country course. There will be a certain amount of dressage, but we shan't concern ourselves with collection or true dressage seats."

"It'll suit Echo," said Henry, "and I'll tell you who'll be particularly pleased, John Manners. He's fearfully worried over Samson. Uncle George, it's a brilliant idea," he went on, his voice gathering enthusiasm.

"I'm glad you approve," said the Major. "Noel looks doubtful."

"I think it's a good idea," answered Noel. "I was just wondering how Tranquil and Truant are going to fit in; I've hardly jumped them at all."

"All the better," said the Major firmly. "In France the young horses are always ridden across country before they're jumped in the school. All this waiting in a queue and then popping over a single jump and going back to the queue is very bad for young horses. Don't get it in your head that you're going to be asked to jump four feet of timber or twelve feet of water, because nothing is farther from my mind.

"Now the next thing is, whom are we going to invite?"

"If I'm the secretary, I'd better make a list," said Henry. He fetched a pencil and paper. "There's Noel and me and John, he's in despair."

"I can't think why you don't all give up riding," said Mrs. Holbrooke. "As far as I can make out the whole Pony Club is in perpetual despair—it seems rather unnecessary."

"Not the whole Pony Club, by any means," Henry corrected her. "Christopher never knows despair."

"Nor does June," said Noel.

"And I don't believe the Radcliffes ever give way to such weaknesses," added Henry.

"Hilary and James might secretly, but I agree that the others wouldn't," said Noel.

"Well, personally I should like a few people who aren't in despair, just to make the course a little more cheerful," observed the Major.

"June and Christopher then," said Henry.

"I don't suppose that June will come," said Mrs. Holbrooke. "She won't be allowed to jump that new hack."

"Well, that's up to her," said the Major.

"How many Radcliffes?" asked Henry.

"Only those of a reasonable age," answered the Major.

"Roger's being very medical at the moment, I shouldn't think he'll come," said Henry.

"Hilary's sure to come if she can and Evelyn may as it's cross-country and not dressage," said Noel.

"Well, invite all three of them. Now who else is there?" asked the Major.

"Oh, Dick, of course," said Henry. "He's been very useful and he's as keen as anyone."

"There are the Hunters," said Noel diffidently, "they're in despair."

"The Hunters? Who are they?" asked the Major.

"Two females with hacked-off blonde hair and enormous goggling eyes," answered Henry promptly. "And we've forgotten Susan." He wrote her name down.

"Are we going to have the Hunters?" asked Noel. "They're terribly bad, but very keen, and Crusoe's nice."

"Of course they've only one horse between them," remarked Henry, "that complicates matters still further."

"Oh, if they're keen let them come," said the Major.

"That's twelve people then," said Henry.

"There's Mrs. Maxton's lot. Aren't any of them good enough?" asked Mrs. Holbrooke. "It seems to me that you ought to make the course more representative of the whole club instead of always having the same people."

"Mrs. Maxton's lot are hopeless. None of her ponies jump an inch," said the Major.

"Of course there are plenty of youthful people like Gay and the younger Mintons, who are quite good."

"I'm not having any eleven- or twelve-year-olds," said the Major. "If they're interested they can come and watch. Miss Sinclair's supposed to instruct them. Now, when do we begin—ten o'clock Monday?"

"Yes, if you'll be strong enough by then. If we leave it much longer some people will go back to school in the middle."

"What about people who live a long way away like Dick and Christopher?" asked Noel. "They won't be able to bring Crispin and William over every day."

"No, but that's quite easy. We can turn the ponies out here and the boys can come over on their bicycles. The secretary has to settle details like that.

"We'll begin with just a couple of hours in the mornings and see how we get on," he continued. "You can work off your surplus energy by lunging each other in the afternoons."

"Surplus energy!" said Henry. "We never have any after being *lunged*, let alone cross-countried. I can think of several people who are going to be in a state of collapse."

"It'll be ghastly if no one can come," said Henry, as he waited for the Barington-Browns to answer their telephone. "Do you think Uncle George would have a course if it were just for us?"

"No," answered Noel. "And if he did we would both collapse with nervous dread and exhaustion long before the end of the week. One needs plenty of people to keep up morale and take turns at being cursed."

Susan could come; she said so at once. "Mummy's so filled with respect for the Major," she explained, "that she never makes any fuss about my going on his courses."

"Who's next?" Henry asked Noel.

"The Radcliffes," answered Noel. "I should ask to speak to Hilary."

Hilary's voice was very loud on the telephone. She said, "Cross-country sounds rather bang on. Look. I'll have to talk it over with the others and Roger's not here at the moment. I'll ring you back to-night."

"Now Dick," said Noel, looking up the number.

Dick was tiresome. First of all he said that the Major ought not to be running a course at all, and when Henry explained that the whole matter had been fully discussed and Mrs. Holbrooke had given way, Dick said that Crispin couldn't make the journey. Henry explained that Crispin was invited to stay, whereupon Dick said that he doubted if he was up to the work; his wind wasn't too good and cross-country sounded strenuous.

It wasn't until Henry had replaced the receiver that Noel thought of Tranquil.

"I could lend Dick a horse," she said.

"It's an idea," said Henry. "Shall I ring him again? If you're certain that you don't mind lending one."

"Positive," said Noel. "Dick's nice to his horses and with the Major about, nothing much can go wrong."

Dick said that Noel's offer was much too generous and she had to persuade him herself before he would accept.

"We're getting on," said Henry, "that's four definite."

John was obviously torn between duty and desire. "It would be at the busiest time of year, that's always the way," he said glumly. "But I must come somehow; it would mean everything to Samson. Tell you what, Henry," he went on after a pause, "I'd better talk it over with Dad and see if we can fix things."

Henry said, "Look, John, if it'd make things any easier you can keep Samson over here. In fact, I might even go so far as to say I'd get him ready for you—I've got used to early rising these last few weeks—then you wouldn't have to be here until five minutes to ten."

John hardly knew what to answer. "That's jolly kind

68

of you," he mumbled in embarrassed tones: "Jolly kind, but wouldn't it be an awful sweat?"

"On the contrary," answered Henry. "When Uncle George's new man starts work on Monday, I'm redundant. I've got to find some use for the enormous muscles I've developed."

"Well, I'll speak to Dad," said John more optimistically, "and let you know to-night."

"Now who's left?" Henry asked Noel.

"Christopher, June and the Hunters."

"Christopher'll come," said Henry, "but I suppose I'd better ring him just to make sure."

Christopher was delighted. "That's super," he said enthusiastically. "Cross-country's just my line. Look, thank the Major for me; especially for saying that he'll have William to stay."

"He knows his own mind, that's one thing," observed Henry. "Now, dare I try the Cresswells?"

"Yes, go on. I hope you get Mrs.," said Noel. "You'll be given a catalogue of every class Silver Splendour's won this summer, if you do."

"We're sure to clash with some fearfully important show," said Henry, dialling the Cresswells' number. "It's not Wembley next week, is it?"

"No, not for ages," replied Noel.

The telephone was answered by June. "A course," she said. "I thought the Major was ill? Oh, he's better, is he? A cross-country course; I can't take Splendour on that, besides I'm going to Crowley Agricultural next Thursday. No, I won't come, thanks."

Henry replaced the receiver. "She was a trifle ungracious, I thought. However, we don't need her."

Before Noel had found the Hunters' number the telephone rang. "Oh, is that Henry Thornton? It's Mrs. Cresswell here." I understand that you rang June just now; something about a course? The poor child was so taken aback to hear of Major Holbrooke's recovery that she didn't know what she was saying. She quite forgot that she has two horses! Of course June'll be there. You know how she is—always ready for anything—and Golden Glory's as hard as nails. There'll just be the one day she won't be able to come, the Thursday. She's riding Silver Splendour at Crowley and, of course, that must come first. Colonel Clintock's judging and he always says that Splendour's a hack in a thousand."

"Right you are," said Henry, as Mrs. Cresswell drew breath. "I'll tell my uncle all about that and we'll see June at ten o'clock on Monday morning. Heaven preserve us from Mrs. Cresswell coming to watch," he said, putting down the receiver. "I didn't know that telephoning could be so exhausting," he added, as he dialled the Hunter's number.

Philippa answered. "Oh, but we're not *nearly* good enough," she protested. "Oh, Henry, we simply *couldn't*. We'd spoil it for all the rest of you. I'm sure the Major can't really want *us*."

Henry held the receiver well away from his ear for Philippa's voice was loud and shrill. He waited patiently with a grin on his face until she had finished speaking, then he said, "Do you want to come or not?"

"Of *course* we should love to come, but Henry—" He interrupted her. "Go and ask your mother if you can," he said firmly, "it begins on Monday at ten o'clock."

"What are they going to do about sharing a horse?" asked Noel.

"I haven't an idea. Persons participating in the course must make a few of their own plans, or the poor secretary will be too worn out to ride himself."

"I hope Philippa won't weep if the Major swears at her," said Noel, "she's rather the type."

"Shush," said Henry, for Philippa was speaking. "Hallo. Yes. You can? That's marvellous. No, I don't care what you do. Can't one watch and the other ride? Well, toss up or something." He rang off. "Now we await the Radcliffes' and John's decisions."

"Seven definites, counting the Hunters as one," said Noel, checking the list. "That's enough, isn't it?"

"Yes, and we're sure to have eight."

"I must go home. I'll just thank the Holbrookes for my tea."

"Well, many thanks for being assistant secretary," said Henry. "I'll see you to-morrow."

"To-morrow's Friday. We've only got three days. Oh dear, I've got the most terrible needle."

"Noel," said Henry in authoritative tones. "That perpetual moaning about the needle is definitely banned; it's all nonsense."

"I *have* got the needle. It's not nonsense. And I'm not Philippa, you can't intimidate me," Noel answered defiantly, as she skipped through the french window.

The soft light of the setting sun had given the sloping lawns a strange luminous green and no breeze stirred the branches of the tall cedars. The Holbrookes were resting on a seat from which you could look down to the ha-ha and across the park.

"I came to say good-bye and thank you very much for my tea," said Noel.

"Dammit!" said Colonel Manners, drinking his after-dinner coffee in the low-ceilinged sitting-room at Lower Basset Farm. "I was given to understand that Holbrooke was half dead and now he just pops up and starts running Pony Club courses as though nothing had happened. He must be made of iron—or mad."

"I think his wife's mad," said Mrs. Manners from the window-seat, where she was darning her husband's and son's socks. "I'm sure that he oughtn't to be running courses after such a terrible accident, but I suppose he's a difficult man to manage."

John wished that parents wouldn't always go off the point. Or hadn't they realised that there was a point?

He looked apprehensively at his father. One had to be so careful with Dad. Often he said "no" to a project just

71

because he was startled by the suddenness of its appearance and then refused to change his mind because he regarded indecision as a weakness.

John decided to chance it. He licked his lips. "Dad," he said, "could you spare me from the farm in the mornings next week? It'll only be half-past nine to lunch-time, because Samson can be stabled at Folly Court and Henry Thornton says he'll do him for me."

The Colonel thought for a moment. "We'll get that wheat in by Saturday, if the weather holds," he said. "Yes, if it doesn't rain between now and Saturday we can spare you. You'd better turn on the wireless and listen to what those meteorological fellas have got to say."

June was furious. "You've made me look a fool in front of that stuck-up Henry Thornton," she told her mother. "I don't want to go and I got myself out of it and then you go and interfere. Anyone could see through all your silly excuses. I jolly well hope Henry tells the Major that you're making me go. Why should I? I hate all the other Pony Club members—they're all either stuck-up or fools—and that fool Glory won't jump a thing and the Major will spend all day picking on me."

"June, really. Hold your tongue," said Mrs. Cresswell. "Of course you will go to Folly Court, I've never heard such nonsense. Glory's a very good jumper and if the other children poke fun at you, you will only have to mention a few of the awards you have won this season to obtain their respect."

June sighed rudely and bit her nails. "Oh, Mummy, you are a fool," she burst out at last. "As if anyone could obtain *their* respect. Why they don't even respect Major Holbrooke; Evelyn Radcliffe always calls him Georgie behind his back."

Mr. Barington-Brown was pleased when he heard about the course. "Just what you need, Susan," he said. "You've been getting that fat and lazy. Do you the world of good to have the Major after you again." Susan giggled. "I expect I shall get into terrible trouble," she said. "I've forgotten the aids for *everything* and Wonder's awfully unschooled. Still, I don't suppose I shall be the worst. Noel's Truant's not a bit well behaved but I expect she'll ride Tranquil, and if John takes Samson and the Hunters' Crusoe I shall be a long way from the bottom."

"Don't you be too sure," said Mr. Barington-Brown. "You've been resting a bit too comfortable on them laurels of yours. One fine morning you'll wake up and find that they've trained those young horses and you're nowhere. Besides, if you can't keep Wonder schooled what's the good of me buying you a young horse?"

"Are you really going to buy me one? When?" asked Susan.

"Well, you can't go on riding that pony forever and you'll need something to ride next summer when you're out of the juvenile classes. But I'm not going to buy you one unless you work on it."

The lounge at March Winds was a very tidy room. One picture decorated the oatmeal coloured walls, no dog lay on the dark blue carpet, no books littered the tables. A television set stood in one corner, a radiogram in another, and the Hunters sat in tidy attitudes on the blue-and-oatmeal speckled chairs.

"But I don't see why we *shouldn't* take it in turns," said Philippa for about the tenth time that evening. "I don't see why the Major *should* mind. I don't believe he's half so fierce and grumpy as the others make out."

"But it would be awful if we enraged him," said Marion. "We might spoil the course for everyone else. You ride, Philippa—you're the eldest—and I'll watch."

"Oh dear, it is *awkward*," sighed Philippa. "If only Henry had been more helpful."

"Don't flop about so, Philippa," said Mrs. Hunter. "All this horse talk leaves me cold. For goodness' sake, draw

73

the curtains, Marion, and let's see if there's anything interesting on the television."

Christopher Minton spent the evening whistling and singing about the house.

"It couldn't be better. A cross-country course. Good old Major; I knew he wouldn't fail us. I wish I were his nephew. I'd get far more out of it than Henry does." But Martin and David had a craze for bagatelle and weren't interested, so he found his mother who was pressing his riding clothes in preparation for Monday.

"Of course, I think the Major gets a bit bored with Henry at times," he told her. "He's had Echo for ages now and I bet William can still beat him at dressage and probably across country too. Of course Echo's a super horse. If he were mine I'd win some hunter classes with him."

Mrs. Minton wasn't really listening to him. "You're not to do any more mucking out in these jodhs," she said. "You must put on your jeans."

"Oh, we've finished with mucking out now," answered Christopher, "the new groom's coming on Monday. We're supposed to sweep the barn up every evening but I generally leave that to the girls—they enjoy doing it."

Dick told his parents about the course when they came down for the week-end with their usual party of smart and famous friends. "I thought it would be too much for Crispin at his age," Dick said, "but I'm being loaned a horse. I think it'll be interesting."

"You take your pleasures so soberly," complained Mrs. Hayward, who was very gay and good-looking and hated the country. "If only it were madly exciting or thrillingly dangerous—but interesting!"

Mr. Hayward, who was a distinguished Q.C., only remarked, "Well, don't let it affect your work," and Dick wished that he had never mentioned it at all.

The Radcliffes discussed the course at dinner.

"Surely the Major oughtn't to be running it?" asked Hilary. "It's fairly energetic swearing and cursing at us."

"Most unwise, I should have thought," said Roger.

Dr. Radcliffe laughed. "I can't altogether agree with my learned colleagues," he said. "Holbrooke's doctor is that old woman Hastings and if *he* let him out of the nursing home I don't think there can be much to worry about."

"Well, that's a relief," said Hilary. "I really felt one ought not to go, but now I think I shall. What about you two?" she asked Evelyn and Roger.

"I think it's jolly mean of him not to allow people of my age," interrupted Margaret. "I can jump just as high as the rest of you. It isn't fair."

Roger said, "I really think I must put work first at the moment."

Evelyn said, "I'm tempted. The thought of the park railings and the hedges at Folly Farm makes one's mouth water. If only one could have the jumps without Georgie Holbrooke. I know it's nice to learn how to do things properly, but he does rant and rave so and this absurd mania for having every little detail perfect...."

"If in doubt, don't go," advised Mrs. Radcliffe. "You really can't go on a course unless you intend to learn."

"It isn't fair on Holbrooke unless you at least *begin* full of enthusiasm," Dr. Radcliffe added.

"But if I don't go I shall be so jealous of Hilary when she comes home and says that she's jumped this and that. And I'm not like Roger; I've nothing else to do."

Noel turned Tranquil and Truant out, put her tack in the little lean-to beside the loose-box and entered Russet Cottage by the back door. In the tiny stone-flagged kitchen that was cool in summer and warm in winter her mother was cooking.

"Oh dear," said Noel. "I'm terribly sorry. I meant to be home early to-night. It's really my turn to cook."

"It doesn't matter a bit. I began early because I felt in a

cooking mood. Dinner's going to be very elaborate and Spanish."

"How lovely. I wouldn't have been so late only the Major decided to run a cross-country course and he asked me to tea to discuss it. Afterwards Henry wanted me to help ring everyone up."

"It sounds as though the Major's feeling himself again," said Mrs. Kettering. "I didn't think he'd be able to sit about doing nothing for long. Which horse are you going to ride?"

"Truant. I'm lending Tranquil to Dick."

"I thought Tranquil was the best behaved."

"Yes, he is, but I can't help liking Truant best."

Friday and Saturday were spent in frantic lunging and schooling by all the members of the course except John who was getting in his wheat and Evelyn who said that she wasn't going to wear herself and her horse out *before* the course. On Sunday the horses rested. Noel helped Henry muck out for the last time. Walker, the new groom, had arrived. On Sunday afternoon John and Christopher hacked their mounts over to Folly Court. Sweet William was turned out and Samson stabled next to Echo.

John was very worried. "You might drum it into the Major just how hopeless Samson and I am," he asked Henry. "Honestly, I should think he'll have a fit when he sees us. The poor old fellow's never had a chance, I mean he's not even fit."

"Oh, you'll be all right," Henry told him. "I'll oat him up like mad and see if I can get you bucked off."

"That reminds me, Dad said I could have the Land-Rover to bring over a couple of sacks of oats. He said we didn't want to eat the Major out of house and home."

Towards evening Henry began to panic. "Aunt Carol," he said, "Uncle George hasn't done a thing about the course yet. Do you think he's forgotten all about it? He must need props of some sort, surely? You can't run a

76

cross-country course on the flat. I was expecting to be put on ditch-digging and hedge-clipping days ago, but nothing's happened at all and it's *beginning* to-morrow."

"My dear Henry, you know I never know anything about these horsy concerns of your uncle's. Go and ask him if he wants anything done, but I've no doubt he would have told you if he did."

"Perhaps I'd better," said Henry, "it would be a fearful catastrophe if he forgot all about it."

He found the Major in the garden.

"Uncle George, is there anything I can do about to-morrow?" he asked. "Do you want jumps put up?"

"To-morrow?" said the Major, looking at him thoughtfully. "No, all we shall want to-morrow is the school; three or four of the old point-to-point flags and a nice piece of rough ground."

"Uncle George," said Henry suspiciously, "what does one do on a cross-country course?"

The Major grinned. "One learns things," he answered, "the like of which you didn't know existed."

CHAPTER SIX

On Monday morning everyone, including Gay, Margaret and James, who had come to watch, was at Folly Court by 9.30. They stood in the yard, discussing Henry's information about the rough ground and the point-to-point flags.

"It sounds to me like a bending race," said Susan.

"It's the limit," Evelyn spoke hotly. "He *can't* call it a cross-country course if we're not going to jump. I shall resign or withdraw or whatever you do."

"Perhaps his head's got worse," suggested Marion.

"No, he seemed sane," Henry told her. "But I don't trust him; he's in one of his whimsical moods."

June said, "I'm not riding Glory over any rough ground; I don't want a sprain, thank you."

"What we need is a drop fence and some water; it won't be a cross-country course without them," said Christopher in dissatisfied tones.

John, leaning dismally against Samson's loose-box door, hoped that there wouldn't be a drop fence or any water because, if there was, he knew who'd be the first to fall in. Noel, sitting on an upturned bucket, felt too weak with the needle to join in the conversation, and Dick was still grooming Tranquil though Noel had groomed him once already.

"9.45," said Henry, looking at his watch. "Everyone had better mount in a leisurely manner and start exercising round the school."

"I'm boiled," said Susan. "I do hope that the Major isn't expecting us to be too energetic."

"If he thinks I'm going to spend the whole morning riding round and round his beastly school, he's mistaken," Evelyn announced loudly. "At the first mention of dressage, I'm off home."

"Do you think Crusoe's bridle's all right, Philippa?" asked Marion anxiously.

"It looks all right to me. Shall I ask Henry?"

"No, you can't bother him," said Marion, as she followed Christopher into the school wishing that she hadn't agreed to ride alternate days with Philippa and that she hadn't lost the toss which had forced her to take first turn.

Everyone began to exercise his horse. Henry crossed his stirrups and trotted round and round with a grim expression on his face. Noel's legs felt too weak for her to copy his example. Her dressage seat had disappeared; she could feel that she was back at all her old bad habits: her hands looked to the withers for support, her eyes seemed glued to the ground.

Christopher was riding at a collected trot; John was kicking Samson; Dick was trying to get the feel of Tranquil, but was hampered by Marion, who would ride on his tail. June and Susan soon stopped riding round; they stood in the centre of the school and discussed Golden Wonder who had once belonged to June.

At exactly ten o'clock Major Holbrooke appeared. He stood at the school gate watching for a few moments before anyone became aware of his presence. Christopher saw him first. "Good morning, Major," he called.

"Good morning, everyone," said the Major, coming into the school. "I should like to say that I am very pleased that you were all able to come on this course and that I hope you will learn a little. I don't know if Henry explained that it was to be a cross-country course, which means we shall concern ourselves only with such school work as is essential for a cross-country horse and we shall spend most of our time in the open."

"Oh goody!" said Susan, and Evelyn muttered, "I should jolly well think so."

"Henry, you'd better lead the ride," the Major went on.

The ten Pony Club members rode their horses round the school at the walk and the Major sat in the middle and gazed at them in critical silence.

At last he spoke. "No dressage seats this week," he said. "For cross-country work you must ride with a cross-country seat. Henry, Noel, John and June, stirrups up two, please. Christopher, Susan, Hilary and whoever that is on the bay horse, up one. Dick and Evelyn, your stirrups are already jumping length. You shouldn't ride with them as short as that normally. You see, instead of acquiring deep seats well down into the saddle you're both sitting on the top and too far back. When you shorten your stirrups you must come forward a little. At the walk you rest lightly on your seat bones—at the trot you rise going forward with your horse; at the canter you stand in your stirrups. I shall call it the Italian canter. Now, reins rather shorter than usual; prepare to trot on. Forward in your saddles and legs back. It's more important than ever that your toe should not be in front of your knee. Change the rein and send the horse on, Henry. We want our horses going forward freely."

They trotted round, the Major criticising everyone's leg position, then he gave the order to canter. Echo shot off with a buck, Quaker was on the wrong leg. Glory was proceeding at her show-ring canter, her head was in the air, her quarters sideways. Truant, Tranquil, Samson and Crusoe were in a bunch on Glory's tail, none of them had cantered a step. Christopher had allowed a gap of several lengths between him and the young horses so the three ponies were able to to canter comfortably.

The Major called the ride to a halt. "That wasn't a very impressive display," he said. "I think I'd better divide you into two rides. Evelyn, you'll lead the second ride. June, you follow her and then the three ponies."

The Major sent Evelyn's ride to canter round while the young horses stood in the centre of the school. Except for telling the riders to shorten their reins and stand in their stirrups, he found little fault with them; he called them in and sent Henry's ride to canter.

They were no better than before.

"Walk, walk," shouted the Major. "Heavens, what an

80

exhibition. Don't you people know *how* to canter? Henry, you must let your horse go *quietly* into the canter. Give a lighter aid and then let him go forward. Don't get hold of him so tightly. The rest of you are all preventing your horses from cantering. Let them go on a bit; drive them forward; leave the reins alone. A young horse will never develop a properly cadenced canter as long as you're hanging on to his head.

"I'm not asking you to canter slowly; Echo isn't cantering slowly; a cross-country horse doesn't need to canter slowly, but he must have a cadence. Now, we'll try again. Take a distance of two lengths between you. Quietly, Henry, give him time."

This attempt was better, they all cantered half-way round the school before they began to bunch. The Major didn't seem very impressed. "Walk," he shouted, and then: "All of you put a short knot in your rein. A knot in the rein, half-way up the horse's neck," he repeated when some of the members looked vague. "Now take the knot in the outside hand. Prepare to canter on. *One* hand, John. Canter on. Sit loosely and drive the horses forward."

It was very hard work. Noel felt as though her legs were about to drop off.

"That's better," the Major was shouting. "Do you feel it? They're beginning to use themselves."

The riders of the young horses were all red in the face with shame and exhaustion when the Major at last told them to walk and then to come in the centre of the school and have a rest while the other ride cantered round. He occupied himself by cursing June, who was still sitting in the back of her saddle with her legs stuck forward and her hands in her stomach.

Henry dismounted and sat on the ground. He wondered whether he would be any better at motor racing. It was absurd to waste so much time and energy in a pastime for which one possessed so little talent.

John sat slumped in his saddle. The Major would

probably give up all idea of the course now he'd seen how badly the horses went. He'll certainly tell me to stick to farming, John thought drearily.

Marion thought, it's terrible. It's even worse than I expected. It's Philippa's turn to-morrow. Perhaps she won't mind it so much. Perhaps I could persuade her to ride every day.

Dick wasn't worried. It's just that Tranquil's a bit green, he thought. I expect I shall get the hang of him."

Evelyn was becoming impatient. It was high time, she thought, that the Major stopped bothering about people's seats and the Italian canter and got on with the jumping. Hilary was feeling pleased with Sky Pilot; he was going jolly well, but Evelyn's rising impatience was spoiling her pleasure just a little; that was the worst of having other members of one's family around, one could feel what they felt and that disturbed one's peace of mind. Still, Evelyn had wanted to come on the course.

Christopher was bored. Oh, come on, he thought, I can do the Italian canter. Let's start jumping. What's the point of bothering with June and holding us all up?

Susan thought, this is *super*, and I haven't been told off once so far so I can't be as bad as all that.

June was furious. I knew this would happen. He's made me look a fool in front of everyone, whatever she says. Who wants to ride at the Italian canter anyhow—the English one's much better.

Major Holbrooke looked round at the dismal faces of the Pony Club members and said cheerfully, "Well, now we'll go outside and do some cross-country work. Noel, you know the sloping field between Little Heath Copse and the Hoghill road, will you lead the way across the fields? I want Henry to drive me."

Noel said, "Which field?" she tried unsuccessfully to visualise a sloping field and Little Heath Copse. "I'm sure I don't know the way there."

"Of course you do. We draw the copse every time Hounds meet at the house."

82

John said, "I think I know the one you mean. It's a permanent pasture again now, but three years ago it was oats and you had to drill it twice because the rabbits had the first lot."

"That's the one. You lead the way then. You can go straight across from the drive—it's all stubble. Hilary, you can lead Echo for Henry. Leave the gates open; we'll soon catch you up. That is if Henry's safe."

The Land-Rover, laden with point-to-point flags, dogs, the younger Radcliffes and Gay Millwood passed the horses and by the time they reached the sloping field the Major and Henry had marked out a course with flags.

"What's the big idea?" Christopher asked Henry, as he came to take Echo. And Evelyn said, "Aren't we *ever* going to jump?"

"Come down into the bottom," Henry answered, "and doubtless my esteemed uncle will unfold his plans."

The Major told them to walk round in a large circle in the same order as they had ridden in the school. "Now," he said, "this is perfectly simple. Do you see the red flag over there on the right? Well, one by one you ride away at a trot outside that flag, turn up the hill outside the two flags on the crest—then turn straight down towards the yellow one, outside that and back here. And the whole exercise is to be carried out at a steady trot. Keep the same pace up and down the hill. Do you all understand?"

"Yes," they answered.

"Right, Henry. Off you go."

Henry started and the Major turned to the other Pony Club members. "Don't forget. Cross-country seats—ride well forward, short reins, keep contact with the legs and reins," he told them. When Henry reached the second flag the Major told Noel to start. She rode away thinking that it looked quite easy, but probably there was some frightful catch. Dick followed Noel and, by the time he started, Henry was coming down the hill. Echo was hurrying rather now that he had turned towards the other horses, but Henry was still riding well forward. "Good," shouted the Major, and told John to start.

Noel was enjoying herself. There was a breeze blowing along the crest of the hill, it fluttered the flags and stirred Truant's mane. It was lovely to be alone with one's horse after being squashed up in the school. Truant tried to slow up as she turned downhill, but she increased the pressure of her legs and he trotted on. She heard the Major shout "Good" as she reached the bottom.

John found he was catching up on Tranquil. "Forward, forward," the Major was shouting at Dick. "Come *on* there. Keep trotting."

Samson was on his forehand. He seemed to be getting more unbalanced at every stride. John was determined to stay forward and keep going, but he was thankful when he reached the bottom in one piece.

The Major was shouting louder than ever. John looked back to see Marion, whose nerves had failed her, coming down at the walk, holding an indignant Crusoe on a tight rein. Evelyn and Quaker were out of control; they came down at a gallop, Quaker's head between his knees, Evelyn leaning back and pulling on the reins. They shot past Crusoe, who gave a light-hearted buck; Marion fell off and Evelyn missed the last flag and, galloping into the group of horses at the bottom, stopped dead. Henry caught Crusoe and Marion picked herself up.

The Major gave Evelyn an angry glare, but he was too busy shouting at June, who was coming down the hill sideways with Golden Glory's head in the air, to give her a lecture.

Christopher, Susan and Hilary all caught up with June and trotted by her before she reached the bottom.

"Heavens," said the Major, when everyone had returned, "this won't do at all. You *must* keep the same pace. It doesn't matter whether you're going up, down or on the level—keep your cadence. It's easy enough; keep the hands steady, put the legs on and ride *forward*. The

84

first two weren't too bad. John, it's useless to pull on the reins when your horse is unbalanced; drive the hocks under him by putting the legs on harder. Dick, coming down you stiffened your knees, stuck your lower leg forward and, consequently, took your weight back. Don't. Keep the legs on the horse; send him forward.

"You," he said, glaring at Marion, "didn't try to do as you were told. I said trot and I meant trot. As for you, Evelyn, you're a disgrace."

"Quaker took the bit between his teeth and he's got a mouth of iron when he wants his own way," Evelyn answered defensively. "Besides, I like galloping downhill and he's not used to trotting."

"No horse has a mouth of iron, and any fool can gallop downhill out of control. Before this week is over we're going to jump downhill at the canter. If you're still riding at that uncadenced pace you'll probably break your neck. But if you get your horse going properly you can jump downhill as safely as on the level.

"June, you must ride forward. In your stirrups. It's easy. Drive the horse forward and get forward yourself. You're using your hands too much and your legs not at all. And to-morrow I want to see that mare in a snaffle. We want a free, happy, supple horse and the snaffle's the bit for that. A dropped noseband will prevent evasions; that is, the horse opening his mouth or crossing his jaw. Few horses pull because their mouths are hard. It's because they are unbalanced and no bit in the world will cure that, only schooling and the rider's legs."

June was looking sulky and, when the Major finished speaking, she said, "I can't hold Glory in a snaffle. She's got a mouth like velvet in a double bridle, but even Wilson can't hold her in a snaffle."

"She doesn't need holding," said the Major sharply. "She needs riding forward. And as for her mouth she hasn't got one—that's what's the matter with her. She never goes near the bit in a double bridle. Look where she carried her head—right up in the air—her back is hollowed and stiff, she doesn't use her hocks and she has no cadence at all.

"Now," he went on in more pleasant tones, "we'll do the same exercise again; only this time—you on the bay horse, what *is* your name?"

"Marion," she answered nervously.

"Well, this time, Marion will go last and John, you go between Noel and Dick."

At the second attempt everyone managed a little better. Henry thought that Echo's cadence was steadier and Noel found Truant less apprehensive about the downhill. John put his legs on as hard as he could and was rewarded by a cry of "Much better." Evelyn trotted down this time, but Major Holbrooke told her that she had been too rough with her hands—all she had to do was to keep the horse going in the cadence, there was no need to start pulling at the reins. Dick's knees had improved and he kept his lower leg back, but he still wasn't riding his horse forward enough and June wasn't riding her horse forward at all but hanging on to the reins and forcing her to come down sideways, which, the Major said, was most dangerous. Marion, mustering all her courage, managed to trot down, but she had reached the bottom in rather a perilous position, half-way up Crusoe's neck. The Major told her that she was much better and went on to explain that the weight of the rider must remain over the stirrups, where it caused least inconvenience to the horse, and not tip forward on the horse's neck, where it would overload his forehand.

"Now the same exercise at the canter," said the Major. "It's no more difficult; just keep your cadence."

"That's easier said than done," observed Henry.

"Canter a circle before you begin," the Major told him. "No, quietly, Henry. Give a *lighter* aid. Of course that horse tears off at the canter. In your stirrups. Slow him up a little. Don't pull, just feel the reins gently. He's beginning to come on the bit." Echo's canter became a little faster as he set off up the hill, and as he turned downhill the speed of it began to increase again.

"Legs," the Major was shouting at Henry. "There you are," he said, turning to the other members as Echo steadied, "that's all you have to do. Right, Noel."

Noel cantered her circle and rode away up the hill. She was really enjoying herself, she decided, and Truant, calm and purposeful, felt as though he was enjoying himself too. She heard the Major shout "Good" as she turned downhill.

John felt hot, but quite happy. He wasn't doing as badly as he had expected and on the whole it was pretty good fun. Don't pull on the reins, he reminded himself as Samson began to lose his balance down the hill.

Dick wasn't sure that he approved of all this tearing down hills. He'd been taught that one should walk a horse down, but he supposed the Major knew what he was doing. He wasn't going to try this out on poor old Crispin anyway. Hallo, here was the third flag. Now, he wasn't to stiffen his knees.

Evelyn was bored. Who cares about cadence, she thought, galloping along the crest of the hill, intentionally gaining on Dick. All this fuss and palaver about how to ride across country, but she betted without taking in a word of it she'd be able to hold her own at the end of the week. Here was the hill. Quaker was beginning to pull, but she liked a horse that took hold. When his speed became too great she sawed at his mouth.

The Major's a fool, thought June, holding Glory back in her slightly sideways show-ring canter, but Mummy's an even bigger fool. I'll make her mad when I tell her about this. I'll make her so mad that she'll ring him up and say that I'm not to come to-morrow. Here was that beastly hill. "Stop it, Glory, stop it, you fool," she said angrily, jerking at the reins. Golden Glory was tired of being held back by niggling hands; she threw up her head, caught June a sharp blow on the nose and galloped down the hill at a fast and uncadenced pace.

"Much better, June, much better," the Major shouted encouragingly. "At least you were straight that time."

Christopher cantered round gaily. His Italian seat felt perfect. William's cadence was excellent. He was enjoying himself but he did hope that the Major wasn't going on and on at this *ad infinitum*. Surely they could have one or two decent jumps? If only they could be divided into two classes. . . . Here was the hill; he cantered down. Really there was nothing in it.

Susan thought, here we go. I shan't be able to stop. What did the Major say about legs? I can't have been listening. Never mind; I don't suppose it matters much. I couldn't stop now to save my life, she thought, as Wonder took charge and galloped full speed down the hill, but really it's super fun.

"Disgraceful," said the Major, as Susan arrived giggling and out of breath. "That is *not* keeping your cadence."

Hilary thought, good old Sky Pilot. This is just your cup of tea; you could keep up this steady pace for hours. The worst of the Major is that he uses so many fancy words like cadence when he could easily say steadily or at a fair hunting pace. I do hope we start jumping soon or Evelyn's going to spend the rest of the day grumbling.

Marion thought, this gets worse and worse. Please God, let Philippa enjoy it to-morrow and then I need never have another turn. Oh, Crusoe, *please* go slowly. Supposing you slipped, you'd be sure to somersault. The Major's shouting, but I can't help pulling on the reins—we're going too fast. It's a hateful feeling.

"Much better," said the Major. "That looked like the Charge of the Light Brigade. Did you enjoy it?"

"No—o. Not much," answered Marion nervously.

"Oh well, you'll get used to it by the end of the week," said the Major heartily. "Now, it's getting on for lunch-time and I think that the riders and horses have probably done enough for the first day. To-morrow we shall begin jumping—but nothing formidable."

"Thank you very much," said the Pony Club members. Henry dismounted and handed Echo to Hilary.

"To-morrow we'll make this course a bit longer," said Major Holbrooke. "There used to be a gravel pit on top of the hill. Drive up there, Henry; I'd like to have a look. I thing it could well be incorporated."

"A Badminton quarry?" asked Henry.

"Yes, but on a much smaller scale."

The gravel pit was overgrown with a tangle of grass, nettles and brambles.

"Just the place," said the Major. "Half an hour with a hook will clear it out. To begin with we can go in down the cart track and out up that steepish place by the tree. Now, drive up there on the left. There was an old point-to-point fence there once and there should be the remains of a ditch."

They found the ditch. It was filled with the birch from the disintegrated fence. "We can soon clear that out," said the Major.

As Noel rode home she thought over the morning. The schooling had been terrible. It seemed such an unjust stroke of fate that she and Henry, who both made such efforts to improve their dressage, should be so much worse than people like Susan, Christopher and the Radcliffes who never appeared to make any effort at all. Of course, they weren't as good as all that. Wonder was always slightly off the bit. Christopher used too much hand; he had a sort of knack of making horses look right. The Radcliffes were tough and rode all wrong, but at least they could make their horses canter.

John unsaddled, watered and fed Samson as quickly as he could, then, mounting his bicycle, he set off for Lower Basset Farm at his fastest speed. He didn't want Dad doing all *his* work.

The Radcliffes and June rode away from Folly Court together.

"Rather a waste of time, I thought," remarked Evelyn, directly they were outside the gates.

"Personally, I enjoyed it," said Hilary, trying to make her voice sound matter of fact.

"Oh, it was quite *pleasant*, I grant you, but what did we do that we couldn't do at home?"

"Quite a bit," answered Hilary, "and to-day was only the beginning; to-morrow we're going to jump."

"Yes, but nothing formidable. That means nothing but beastly, potty little jumps of two-foot-six. Old Georgie Holbrooke simply panders to all the nervous wrecks nowadays. What do you think of it, June?"

"He's a fool," answered June. "What's the point of making the horses gallop up and down those hills? It only wears their tendons out. I hope that Mummy says I needn't come any more when I tell her what happens."

"It wouldn't surprise me if Marion packed up too," observed Evelyn. "She hasn't the nerve for it either."

June scowled malevolently.

"I'm not afraid, if that's what you're hinting at," she said. "It's all very well for people with common old slugs to go galloping all over the place, but if you've got a decent, well-bred horse like Glory no one but a fool wants to hot it up or ruin its legs."

"Are you suggesting that Quaker and Sky Pilot are common old slugs?" asked Evelyn.

June looked at her; cold, pale, pebble-like eyes gazing into Evelyn's eyes of turbulent green.

"If the cap fits, wear it," June said, and kicking Glory into a trot she clattered away up the road.

"The things I'd like to do to that girl," said Evelyn furiously, and then turning on the silent Hilary, "I suppose you enjoy hearing our horses called common old slugs?"

"No, I don't, but you started the row by saying that June was nervous."

"Well, she is. Look at the way she rode downhill."

"There was no need to say so."

"I believe in saying what I think," said Evelyn.

"Well, dear?" asked Mrs. Cresswell inquiringly, as soon as June reached Dormers.

June scowled as she dismounted. "I've got to take Glory in a snaffle to-morrow," she said, a faint note of triumph in her voice, "the Major says she's got an awful mouth. We spent most of the morning galloping up and down a hill full of rabbit holes and neither Evelyn nor Marion Hunter could stop; they charged about everywhere and nearly knocked Glory over."

"June, what is all this? What are you saying?" asked Mrs. Cresswell in a horrified voice.

"Oh, Mummy, can't you listen?" asked June rudely. "I said that the Major said that Glory had an awful mouth and was to go in a snaffle to-morrow."

"Never! June, I don't believe a word you say. You're simply making this up. Glory has a mouth like velvet."

"That's just what I told the Major," said June smugly. "He shouted like a madman and said that she had no mouth at all. You should have heard him."

"Perhaps he isn't quite recovered from his accident. Did he seem strange in other ways, June?"

"If you mean balmy, I should jolly well think he is. Just fancy finding a hill full of rabbit holes and making people ride up and down it all morning. I didn't want a sprain, thank you. I took it jolly slowly; you should have heard him shouting at me to go faster. All the same, I shan't be a bit surprised if Glory pulls out lame."

"Oh dear; really it's too bad."

"Well, I suppose I'd better tell Wilson to find a snaffle for to-morrow," said June, in resigned tones. "I should think it'll be the end of Glory's legs. Unless I keep her well collected, how can I avoid the rabbit holes? And even Wilson can't hold her in a snaffle."

"Now wait a moment, June. I can't have you going tomorrow until I've gone deeper into this. I shall ring up Major Holbrooke."

"Oh Mummy, you are a fool," said June. "You'll only have another row."

Henry had spent a peaceful afternoon in the gravel quarry alternately hacking at brambles and nettles with a slasher and lying on his back in the shade. At tea-time he wandered back to Folly Court feeling virtuous. His aunt and uncle were eating tea, which was laid beneath one of the cedars on the lawn.

"The troubles' begun already," said the Major cheerfully, as Henry sat down. "Mrs. Cresswell rang up."

"Lord preserve us," said Henry. "What did *she* want?"

"I never quite made out what she wanted, but it seemed that June had rushed home with many tales to tell. First of all did I really mean that Glory was to wear a snaffle tomorrow. I said yes, very firmly, I explained that it was a cross-country course and I gave her a little talk on the different position of the horse and the lesser degree of collection that we required. She informed me that Glory had a mouth like velvet and I said that it was certainly the sort of mouth customary among show hacks, but that for cross-country riding something rather different was needed. I really kept my temper admirably, didn't I, darling?" said the Major, turning to his wife.

"You did. To tell you the truth, you sounded so unlike yourself I considered telephoning for Dr. Hastings."

"Well then," the Major went on, "she seemed quite happy about the snaffle, but she began talking about rabbit holes and whether it wasn't rather risky. I said that if June had seen any she should have pointed them out to me and then I could have had them filled in. After that Mrs. G. became horribly effusive. She said how glad she was that she'd telephoned me and what a lovely chat we'd had. She went on for hours."

CHAPTER SEVEN

"Oh stop it, Glory," said June, as she struggled with the stud billets of her bridle in the yard at Folly Court on Tuesday morning. "Stand still, you fool."

"What's the matter?" asked Susan. "Oh, I'd forgotten that you've got to ride in a snaffle. Won't it undo?"

"Haven't you got eyes?" Susan giggled. "I'm hopeless at undoing stud billets."

"If only this fool would keep still," said June.

"Everyone in the school, please," called Henry. Golden Glory became even more excitable. As the other horses were ridden away she began to drag June round the yard. Henry came back to see what was the matter.

"Oh lord, your snaffle. Look, put the 'orse in the box and take the bridle right off. Here, you hold Echo and let me have a try." Henry didn't take long to undo the bits, and just as he got them off Noel appeared.

"If you'll hold Truant too, I'll help Henry," she said to June, "the Major's waiting."

"Well, *he* wants me to ride in a beastly snaffle."

"Have you got a dropped noseband?" asked Henry.

"No," June told him, "and I don't want one either."

"Well, my esteemed uncle said that you were to borrow one of his, so you'd better." Leaving Noel to adjust the bit, he ran to the saddle room to fetch a noseband.

When June was ready they rode to the school. The Major was sitting on his shooting stick apparently taking no notice of anyone. Philippa was riding round with Dick telling him that she didn't feel the least bit nervous though she had expected to be quite terrified. Susan was sitting sideways on Golden Wonder and giggling with Margaret, James and Gay. John, Christopher and Hilary were schooling busily.

"Sorry we're late, Uncle George," said Henry, "but June's bridle got stuck."

"That's all right," answered the Major. "You'd better ride those horses in before we begin." Henry crossed his stirrups and began to trot round with a grim expression on his face. Noel's needle became over-powering; Truant wouldn't go forward properly; he'd lost all his impulsion. Oh dear, she thought, pushing him into a trot, we're going to be even worse than yesterday.

After a few minutes the Major spoke. "I'm sorry to say that none of you has the least idea of how to ride a horse in. I know that most of them have been hacked over here, but even so, they are coming into a strange school among a crowd of strange horses, they are bound to be apprehensive and therefore stiff. Now the whole purpose of riding a horse in is to get him to relax. As long as your horse is stiff you cannot get the best out of him either in dressage or jumping, and however well schooled and supple a horse is, he is not relaxed enough to begin schooling when you first mount. This morning Echo's back is extremely stiff and that makes it more or less impossible for Henry to sit in the saddle. However he's a very determined character so he sits down hard, sets his teeth, grips with everything he's got, and stiffens *himself* in his efforts to stay in the saddle. The stiffer you become, Henry, the stiffer Echo will be—it's a vicious circle.

"Christopher has a different approach. He says, 'Here you, I like a nice collected horse.' He puts the legs on. He takes a firm feel on the reins, setting his hands so that they work like a tight side rein. 'Come on, William,' he says, 'Nose in.' William says that he's stiff, but Christopher tells him to snap out of it and bring his nose in. I know that to the unpractised eye, he looks right. His nose is in, his neck is pleasantly arched, he is shortened, but it isn't right. You'll find that out when come to your more advanced work, Christopher.

"Don't try to get hold of your horses. First of all ride round on a long rein at the walk. Keep the horse going forward and wait for him to relax. You should, provided you are supple yourself, be able to feel him swinging his back. Then pick up your reins, but don't try to get hold of him, and ride either at the trot or canter, whichever is your best pace. Put the legs on, keep a light contact and wait for the horse to come on the bit.

"Directly you try to get hold of him he'll stiffen somewhere and then he can't come on the bit, because if he's stiff he can't bring his hocks under him. Do you all understand?"

"I think," said Henry doubtfully, "that I have an inkling."

Christopher said, "But I do ride on a loose rein first, before I try to collect him. I ride round several times and then I start collection."

"Well, don't," answered the Major, "go on riding round and wait for the horse to come on the bit.

"Now, walk on round. We're going to try to put some of these horses on the bit. Take a light contact with the mouth and put your legs on. I said a *light* contact, John. Take a firm contact and you defeat your own ends; it is the horse which must strengthen the contact, not the rider. Prepare to trot on."

The Pony Club members rode round for a time, the Major finding faults with everyone. They changed the rein, and the two rides rode on two circles. The Major was far from satisfied. At length he halted them. "This is no use," he said. "I'll have to take you each in turn. Henry, trot a circle in that half of the school."

Henry and Echo trotted a circle, but it wasn't smooth or pleasing to the eye; they seemed at variance with one another. The Major watched in silence and then he said, "Go with him a little more, Henry. You're trying to get behind him too much. That's better. Now," the Major said, turning to the other Pony Club members, "you can see the point of riding the horse on the circle when you're trying to get him on the bit. Henry can ask for a much more powerful trot without Echo going too fast because

95

the circle helps to regulate the pace. One develops the horse's quarters by drive, but one must regulate the speed by tact, otherwise the lesson will degenerate into a pulling match.

"Come on, Noel. Your turn," said the Major.

Noel put on her legs so hard that Truant shot out of the line of horses in surprise.

"Steady, steady," said the Major disapprovingly. "Now, trot a circle, but do try to begin quietly."

Noel was driving and going forward with Truant, but he looked unhappy, he was off the bit and not going nearly as well as he did across country.

The Major watched. And then at last he said, "Try to relax your arms, Noel. Your upper arms should hang by your sides and your elbows should be relaxed and springy. Bend at the elbow. Yes, that's better. Did you feel how he lowered his head and went on the bit? Relax again. There, you see; he's quite a different horse. Change the rein and go on relaxing your elbows."

John was ready when his turn came. "Now this horse is rather more difficult," the Major said, as he began to circle. "He's very green and he's a big horse and rather loose limbed." John, who had only trotted round twice, was already red in the face with exertion when the Major said, "Stop driving a minute. Just let him trot round and try and feel how he goes. He's got a very slow cadence this horse, and you're driving him out of it." John looked very mystified but he sat still and it became obvious to everyone that Samson flopped just as much whether John was driving or not. "Now," said the Major, "try and fit your driving in with his trot. We don't want him to go any faster, we want to develop his quarters so that he can carry himself. Leave the reins alone, they won't help you. It sounds odd," Major Holbrooke went on, "but one uses one's legs more on an impetuous horse than on an idle one. An impetuous horse gains confidence in the legs if they are always against him, whereas an idle horse respects them more if they are used less but more energetically. All right, John, that's

96

much better. You can't expect to get him right in five minutes, but he's improving."

Dick rode his circle pleasantly and peacefully. But the Major pointed out that Tranquil wasn't on the aids. "You see, your legs are slightly too far forward again," he explained, "and consequently your horse isn't between the hand and leg nor is he on the bit. I know he's going quite nicely at the moment, but you'd find that a tricky combination of fences would be your undoing, because a horse which isn't on the aids cannot be shortened or lengthened quickly—the aids just don't go through him. Relax your knees a bit more—that will enable legs to come closer to the horse.

"Now, who's next?" asked the Major, looking round. "Ah, yes, Marion," he said, with an air of triumph at remembering the name. Philippa smiled brightly at him and, giving Crusoe a kick, began to trot round.

"Walk a minute; that's no use—you've got the horse bent the wrong way."

"Oh dear, I'm so sorry," said Philippa. "Perhaps if you could just show me which way he *should* be bent . . ."

"That is what I intend doing," answered the Major. "You know that when a horse is on a straight line his body should be straight and follow that line and that when he is in a curved line his body should be curved?"

"Yes, I think I just know that," answered Philippa.

"Well then, turn his head in a little, so that you can see his inside eye. Put your inside leg on the girth, your outside leg behind it and give a little with your outside hand."

"Now what do I do next?" asked Philippa with a bright smile, when she had arranged her hands and legs.

The Pony Club members were beginning to giggle. "Trot round on the circle," said the Major. "And *don't* kick," he shouted, as Crusoe leapt into a trot. Philippa pulled up abruptly, "I've been meaning to ask you about kicking. Is it really so naughty and why?"

"Kicking isn't horsemanship. It's rough and untidy. It

97

D

upsets impetuous horses and makes slugs of quiet horses. It takes your legs off the horse at crucial moments. If you ride properly, with your legs against the horse, he will be on the bit, ready to obey a light aid, and there will be no need to kick."

The Major was obviously tired of Philippa; he only let her trot round once and then he asked who was next. Evelyn was; she wouldn't sit loosely and give Quaker a chance to come on the bit. She kept his hocks under him and he was full of life, but always above the bit.

"Your horse doesn't understand the bit and isn't in a position to obey it," the Major told her. "That's why you have to use those rough rein aids to turn and stop."

Evelyn said that she understood; but in a voice that made it obvious she didn't mean to do anything about it. The Major looked at her for a moment and then, apparently deciding to say nothing, called for June.

"You've only got to remember one thing, put your legs against the horse and keep them there. Don't kick; just put the legs on harder until she trots. Good. Now take your reins a little shorter. That's right. She's beginning to come."

Christopher, watching the other members riding their circles, had come to the conclusion that they all let their horses slop. I'll show them how it ought to be done, he thought as he began to trot round.

"You're setting your hands," said the Major. "Loosen up a bit; take a slightly longer rein. Now, give him the chance to put himself on the bit."

William cut in towards the centre of his circle.

"That's what happens when I ride him without a contact," said Christopher grumpily.

"He cuts in because he's not on the bit," the Major explained. "Use your inside leg more; try to make the circle larger."

"But if I ride him like I usually do he doesn't cut in," objected Christopher. "Look." Taking a firm contact with

98

William's mouth he turned his head in and held him in position with the reins.

"Yes, I know you can do it like that, but it's not the right way. The pony is stiff, he loses his impulsion. It would be one thing to ride like that if you were going in a test tomorrow and hadn't time to correct his position, but it is absurd not to try to correct it while you're schooling at home. That pony hasn't much of a trot and it's never going to develop as long as you hold him so tightly."

Susan and Hilary both held their ponies too tightly. When they lightened their contacts and began to use their inside legs at the appropriate moments, their ponies began to go better.

"There you are," said the Major, when Hilary had finished, "you've seen for yourselves how the horse's neck becomes longer, how he stretches himself forward and goes on the bit. You've only got to put the legs on, take up the lightest of contacts and wait for the horse. If you do your basic training properly the horse will go on and on improving. As his muscles develop so will his balance and carriage. His paces will become more powerful, his appearance more impressive and you will find him executing the movements you have taught him with greater and greater ease.

"Well, that's enough schooling. Form up the ride; take a distance of two lengths. Will the spectators be kind enough to bring one of those Cavalletti . . ."

James and Gay carried in a Cavalletti.

"Put it here," said the Major. "Ride, turn down the centre of the short side. Ignore the Cavalletti, trot over it as though it wasn't there."

Echo wouldn't ignore the Cavalletti; he broke into a canter and cleared it with a flying leap.

Truant approached with caution, stepped over gingerly and fled in horror. Samson was more sensible, he trotted over merely increasing his stride. "Good," said Major Holbrooke.

Tranquil wasn't attending, he stumbled as he trotted over. Crusoe ran out. "What do you think you're doing?" demanded the Major.

He roared at Evelyn for kicking Quaker on the take-off and causing him to jump.

"Sit still," he shouted at June, who was steering with the reins. "Sit still," at Christopher, who was flapping his legs. "Keep still," at Susan, who threw herself forward, and at Hilary whose hands shot up Sky Pilot's neck. He turned round to halt the ride and failed to see Philippa run out at her second attempt.

"Now look," he said, "you're all doing far too much. Let the *horses* jump. Not that this is jumping but the principle is the same. Put the horse on the bit and then sit still and see what happens. Don't disturb your horse by making all these violent movements; just follow him. Trot on again; Marion, go last and don't run out."

They trotted over the pole several times with the Major criticising everyone's seat, and then he asked the spectators to place another Cavalletti about four feet from the first. "Don't do anything," the Major told the Pony Club members, "the horses will stride over and this exercise causes them to lower their heads and round their backs, which is the position we want for jumping. Keep your trot active all the time."

Echo was convinced that two Cavalletti made a jump. Each time he approached them he flung his head into the air, cantered and leaped over. "Go and ride behind Hilary," the Major told Henry, when his earlier advice, to sit still and lean back a little, had failed to have any effect. "Ride on her tail."

Echo still hadn't trotted over the Cavalletti properly when it was time to go outside.

"Ride out to the field quietly," said the Major, "and then dismount and give the horses a few minutes' rest. I shan't be long. I'm just going to have a cup of coffee. I'll get Jeffrys to drive me over, Henry, I want him to clear out that ditch."

"Goodness, I'm hot. I could do with a drink too," said Susan, "but not coffee. Ugh, I hate the stuff."

"Where's the nearest shop which sells ice-cream?" asked Christopher.

"Miles away; practically in Brampton."

"Well, James has got nothing to do, why doesn't he bicycle in and get us all some?"

"Why should he?" asked Evelyn. And Susan said, "Honestly, Christopher, it's miles and it would all be melted by the time he got back."

"Oh well, I suppose I shall have to make do with a drink from the tap," grumbled Christopher.

"You can have some of my lemonade if you like."

They rode into the yard and everyone began to produce bottles and offer them round.

"Hurry, hurry, hurry," yelled Henry. "The interval for refreshments is now over. Come on, Noel," he continued more quietly, "perhaps if we start, they'll stop swilling minerals and follow."

Noel mounted. "Oh dear," she said, "I drank some of Susan's fizzy stuff and now it's doing the most peculiar things inside me."

"How very ill-advised of you. Never mind, Uncle George's quarry is guaranteed to cure hiccups."

"Oh you beast. Now you've brought on my needle," wailed Noel.

As they rode across the drive John joined them. "This blasted weather's all very well for the harvest, but it's not what I'd choose for riding," he said. "At least, I suppose it might be O.K. before breakfast."

"That's enough of that," said Henry. "You are not to go putting such ideas about. Three hours of Uncle George before breakfast is *not* my idea of a good time. What *are* the others doing?" he asked June and Dick, as they came trotting up.

"Fooling around as usual," answered Dick. June said, "It's Christopher again. He drank all Gay's raspberryade and then he wanted Margaret's bottle. They were chasing about and shrieking like anything."

"Oh curse them," said Henry.

"They'll come," said Dick, "and after all, the Major's coffee will take several minutes to drink."

"Philippa, Susan and the Radcliffes are coming now," said June, "that's everyone but Christopher and it serves him right if he's late."

Christopher appeared at the canter just as everyone else had reached Little Heath field and was debating whether to inspect the quarry. His face was red, his shirt torn. "That little beast, Margaret. She's ripped my shirt to glory," he complained to Henry. "I can't *think* why your Uncle George lets her come."

"I can't *think* why he lets the rest of us come up here," answered Henry. "You can't really describe any of us as ornamental."

"She's got no manners at all," Christopher continued angrily. "She needs to be taught a lesson."

"No more incidents with rakes if you don't mind."

"That was her own fault. I don't blame myself a bit."

"You'd better dismount and look as though you'd been here for some time."

"Oh, the Major wouldn't mind. We understand each other."

"Have you shown them the quarry?" the Major asked Henry, as the Land-Rover stopped beside the horses. "No." "Well, show them where you go in and the place beside the trees where you come out. We're going to include it in yesterday's course. There's nothing to it; you simply keep the horse's cadence and your own position. I'm just going to show Jeffrys the ditch."

The mounted party inspected the quarry and then the Major sent them down to the valley with instructions to come at the trot in the same order as they had the day before. He stayed on the top of the hill.

Henry began and soon the horses were strung out across the hillside; they were not pulling or passing each other

102

to-day, but trotting on steadily. The quarry caused no trouble. Some of the horses were a little apprehensive about entering it, but none made any fuss about scrambling up beside the tree. When everyone had been round at the trot the Major told them to canter. Except that Glory and Crusoe trotted down the hill and Quaker and Evelyn pulled at each other, the horses went well.

"This is enormous fun," said Henry, as they waited for the Major's next orders. "There's nothing like cantering downhill when your horse is going well."

"And the quarry too," said John. "It's a jolly good idea."

"It's a lovely feeling, cantering on and on like that with no one in the way," remarked Noel.

Henry said, "Uncle George is making strange gestures. I think perhaps he wants us up there."

"Excellent," said the Major, when they joined him. "A great improvement. Now the ditch is ready and I want you to trot over one behind the other. Two lengths distance and let the horses do the jumping."

The ditch was about two feet six wide and about two feet deep. Echo refused it and then, on second thoughts, jumped from a standstill. Truant assumed an expression of horror and refused to approach it.

"Keep your legs on," said the Major. "Give him a bit more rein. Don't tip forward when your horse stops; take the weight back a bit, sit up. Drive him forward. Go on, right up to the brink. Good. Now pat him. It is useless," he went on, turning to the other members, "to take a horse back for a second attempt until he has signified his willingness to jump by going right up to the obstacle. All right, Noel, have another try."

Truant refused again and the Major told Noel to stand on one side until he had found someone to give her a lead. Tranquil had one refusal, but the second time Dick rode at the ditch he used his legs and whip and heels and scrambled over somehow.

"Gently," said the Major, "you don't want to force the
103

young horses, you want them to gain such confidence that they carry you over."

Samson didn't notice the ditch until the last moment, then he refused and nearly slithered in.

"Let him have a look. Don't get excited. You rode him a bit too hard; you pushed him right out of his natural cadence. Wait a minute and you can have a lead."

Evelyn and Quaker jumped the ditch from a canter, and then Glory put on one of her nappy acts.

"Take a slightly shorter rein," said the Major. "Now trot her round on a large circle driving her well on the bit. Good. Keep going like that. Turn, and ride over the ditch." Glory jumped the second time and the three experienced ponies followed her without any fuss, but Crusoe refused and Philippa fell off.

"This time, sit still," the Major told her, when she had remounted. "Don't jump before the horse does."

Then the Major reorganised the ride so that each of the young horses had an experienced horse to follow. He told Hilary, who was leading, to keep trotting over the ditch and to ride round on a really big circle so that everyone could keep going and there need be no slowing down or bunching. When the horses were following each other over the ditch with complete confidence, the Major told the ride to change the rein and canter on.

The horses jumped well; even Quaker had stopped pulling, and when everyone had jumped the ditch three times at the canter the Major halted the ride.

"Well, that's *much* better," he said. "There's already a big difference in the way that some of the horses are going; I hope that you're pleased with them."

"Yes," John spoke first, "I jolly well am."

The others muttered in agreement.

"That will do for to-day then. Henry, you and I will have to put some work in on the fences this afternoon."

"Can some of the others come back and help if they want to?" asked Henry.

"Of course they can," said the Major. "The more the better, provided that they're prepared to work."

"Oh goody," exclaimed Susan, "I love making jumps."

Nearly everyone said that they would come back to help, but after lunch only Susan, Noel, James and Gay turned up; the others had all found the lure of swimming or tennis too great, or the thought of a bicycle ride too uninviting.

"Never mind," said Henry, when he found the depleted band sitting on the plot of grass in the middle of the yard. "It's really much nicer if there aren't too many of us, we should only squabble over the hammer."

"I've brought my gimlet and screwdriver," said James. Henry grinned. "A gimlet isn't going to get through the posts and rails Uncle George is laying on," he said. "They're nearly as tough as the timber they use at Badminton, but as a special concession to our youthful necks they're not to be bolted together, but tied with string."

"Oh shut up," said Noel, "you've brought my needle on again."

CHAPTER EIGHT

ON Wednesday morning the people who had spent Tuesday afternoon building the course were able to assume a very superior attitude towards the people who hadn't come to help.

"We had a simply super time," Gay told Margaret. "You've no idea—James and I did all the hole-making with a brace and bit, and the Major said that we'd been a great help. He asked us all to tea and I think Folly Court's the wizardest house I've ever been in."

"I know, I know. James told me all about it. I couldn't be fagged to come all that way back."

Marion, who, much against her will, was having her turn, was perturbed to hear about the new jumps.

"Are they *very* big?" she asked nervously.

"*Enor*mous," Henry told her. "The log in the quarry's four feet and there's a post and rails which is every bit of three feet nine. The drop fences are terrific."

"Oh, Henry, you are a liar," said Susan, with a giggle. "Don't believe a word he says," she told Marion. "None of them is over two feet six."

"Oh lord, I thought that we were going to get some decent jumps at last," said Christopher crossly. "Couldn't you have banged them up a bit, Henry?"

"They're fairly tricky," Henry told him, "I shouldn't underestimate them. Uncle George has been devilish ingenious in his placing of them."

"Oh well, if they're tricky they sound just the thing for William," said Christopher complacently.

"I'm sure I shan't be able to do them at all," said Marion, wrinkling her forehead in anxiety.

"Neither shall I," Noel told her, "so you won't be the only one. I'm expecting to fall into the ditch, which now has a brush fence attached to it, refuse the quarry and fall flat at the drop fences."

"Stop creating alarm and despondency," said Henry. "Ignore her," he told Marion. "She goes on like this and then, when her turn comes, she clears the lot."

"Liar," said Noel.

John appeared at five minutes to ten looking very harassed. "One of the cows had to go and calve," he explained. "it put us all behind hand. Oh, you've saddled and bridled him. That's decent of you, Henry."

"A pleasure," answered Henry, "and, despite your mid-wifery, you're not the last; June hasn't turned up yet, but I think I hear her hoofs."

"I'm just about cooked," John complained as he mounted. "It must be hotter than ever; do you think the Major would mind if we took our ties off?"

The Major did not seem to be in the least affected by the heat; in fact, his energy seemed to have increased. He made the Pony Club members ride at an active trot until they nearly collapsed with exhaustion.

"There's no point at all in riding sloppily," he told them severely when they began to groan and mutter, "only active paces can develop muscles. It is better to ride actively for a short time and then to dismount and take a rest than to go on and on when you're tired and the horse is going badly."

"Can we have a rest now?" asked Christopher.

"Very well. If you feel you need it, everyone can dismount for five minutes."

The Pony Club members sat on the ground and grumbled about their legs; the Major lit a cigarette.

"When you are recovered," he said, "we're going to do some shoulder-in. I think there are quite a few people here who haven't attempted it before so I'll explain what we want. Shoulder-in is a school movement and its pur-pose is to supple the horse. It can be ridden on two tracks but at first we ride on three tracks. Suppose that you are going to ride shoulder-in along that side of the school. As you come round the corner from the short side you will increase the horse's cornering position and then keep him in that position as you proceed along the straight. In other words, his head, neck and inside shoulder will be bent to the inside, his inside foreleg will be off the school track, his inside hindleg will follow in the track of the outside foreleg, and his outside hindleg follows a track of its own. The horse's head is flexed in the opposite direction to the movement. As you know, in Passes, Renvers and Travers the horse must look in the direction in which he is going. His head leads the movement and is bent and flexed in that direction, but in shoulder-in he is bent and flexed in the opposite direction.

"You all know the aids for riding round a corner or on a circle. Apply them. Increase the pressure of the muscle leg. Can you show us, Henry?"

"After a fashion, but it's not a very inspiring sight."

"William can do it," said Christopher eagerly.

Henry rode down the long side of the school at shoulder-in. "Yes," said the Major, when he had finished, "the position was good, but you hadn't enough impulsion. Give him a short trot, then bring him back to the walk just as you come round the corner, and you should have some impulsion with which to begin the movement. Directly you feel that you're losing your impulsion ride forward again. Good. Now, Christopher. Yes, your position is good, but you've no impulsion at all; you're holding that pony too tightly."

One by one the Pony Club members attempted shoulder-in. No one did as well as Henry, but they all managed to produce some semblance of the movement.

"You all have the same fault," the Major told them, "you will use too much rein. Use less rein and more inside leg. You are having to force the movement too much. Try to make it look easy. Change the rein. We'll see what you're like to the other side. Now take up your position as you come through the corner. Don't carry the inside hand to the outside—the hands must always remain on their own sides of the withers. Just turn your shoulders to the centre of the school, that gives you the rein aid; now it's the inside leg on the girth."

When they had done with shoulder-in, they started Cavalletti work. All the horses, except for Echo and Crusoe, were trotting over the poles well, but Samson was the best and John was very pleased and patted him endlessly. The Major said that Tranquil, Truant and particularly Glory were greatly improved and made everyone watch them striding over the Cavalletti with lowered heads, rounded backs and serious expressions.

When Echo had jumped into the middle of the Cavalletti three times and Crusoe had alternately tripped over them and run out, the Major said that everyone except Marion and Henry could dismount and have a rest. He had the third Cavalletti taken away and then told Marion and Henry to ride over the remaining two. They could do this at the walk but at the trot it defeated them.

"Come on," said the Major. "This is the moment to use your brains. They're your horses, and you've got to explain to them what you want. It's no use thinking that they won't do it, because all horses will do Cavalletti work the moment they understand what we want."

"You know more horse language than I do," said Henry. "My vocabulary doesn't run to this."

"Well," said the Major, "your horse is shortening his stride and hurrying as he comes up to the Cavalletti. We want him to lengthen it so that he can stride over. Can you think of a reason for him shortening his stride?"

"Presumably too much rein would make him shorten."

"Yes. I think that Echo is worried over the poles so, as he draws near he begins to hurry—he wants to get it over. When he hurries, you shorten up the reins and then he can't lower his head or round his back and he becomes more worried. You must try to explain that there's nothing to worry about. You can do that by being relaxed in your seat, arms and hands. Encourage him to lengthen his stride, more leg and keep the hands quiet. Go and give him a trot round now. Keep your legs on, give with your hands, take your weight back when he begins to hurry." To Henry's surprise and delight Echo trotted over the Cavalletti.

"Pat him," said the Major. "Keep going and come again. Marion, follow Henry and *push* with your legs."

When Henry and Marion had both ridden over the Cavalletti twice without a mistake, the Major asked the spectators to bring two jump stands and a pole into the school. He arranged a small jump of about two feet about eight yards from the two Cavalletti.

"Now, sit still, treat the little jump as though it were another Cavalletti; keep your legs on the horse and let him carry you over. Lead on, Henry, at the trot."

All the horses, except for Glory, who knocked the jump down, managed this exercise quite calmly and, when everyone had had three turns, the Major said that it was time to go outside.

There was no loitering in the yard this time; everyone was eager to see the course and they rode out at a much faster pace than the official walk. However, Henry, becoming used to the Land-Rover, was driving faster and they were still inspecting the uphill jump or giving cries of horror over the quarry when the Land-Rover arrived.

"Come on, we don't want to waste time," called the Major to the scattered riders.

They began with the fence and ditch. The Major told the riders of the young horses to follow the people who had given them leads the day before. They trotted round in a large circle until the horses were going with their heads low and stretching on the bit. "Right, Henry," called the Major. "Follow on, everyone. Keep your distance. Dick, your legs aren't on; your knees are stiff again. Evelyn, your legs aren't on; put them back and get your weight forward. June, shorten your reins." Echo broke into a canter and threw himself at the fence. "Give with your hands," roared the Major.

No one refused. Samson and Truant thought of doing

so, but their riders' legs were close to them and they changed their minds and jumped. Crusoe took charge of Marion; he cantered at the fence and carried her over. She took a firm hold of the mane.

"Good," said the Major. "That horse's confidence is coming back. You sit like you did then and let him get on with the jumping.

"Round again. Keep on trotting," the Major was shouting. "Stop gossiping. Keep those horses going at the same steady pace. There's forty acres here, Henry, make the circle bigger. Now relax as you come up to the fence, pat that horse, leave the reins alone. Good. You see, the horse relaxed too."

The third time round, they jumped the fence and ditch at the canter and then the Major led the way to the uphill and downhill fences, which were on the same slope at the same level, but at some distance from each other.

"Now, this is perfectly simple. The ride will stand here. The first person will trot down, jump the downhill jump *from a trot* and continued *straight* down to the bottom of the hill, ride along the valley, turn up, jump the uphill fence and trot back here. Is that clear?"

"Yes," answered the Pony Club members.

"Good. Now it is imperative that the horse's head should be low and that he should jump quietly and calmly when going downhill. To do this he must be under easy control, not pulling or fighting, but balanced and on the bit. Use plenty of leg and seat; keep your hands light and tactful. Coming uphill ride well forward and sit still; give the horse plenty of rein. Right, Henry."

Henry trotted a circle and then rode downhill. Echo looked at the fence, he took it steadily and jumped well. The uphill was nothing to him.

Dick was rather out of control.

"You took your legs off *again*," the Major told him, when he returned. "Then, when you found the horse was becoming unbalanced, you shortened your reins, but that's not the right way to correct a loss of balance."

June lost her head altogether. She stuck her legs forward and hung on to the reins. "Some people want to kill themselves," muttered the Major in between roaring advice at her.

Evelyn rode down recklessly and came back looking pleased with herself, but the Major only remarked that it was a pity that her skill didn't match her courage.

Christopher was told that he was very good, and Noel that she wasn't too bad at all.

Golden Wonder took both the downhill and uphill fences calmly and Susan rode back patting her enthusiastically. Samson stopped at the downhill fence the first time, but the Major said that he had shown sense as he had realised that he was coming at it wrongly. He told John to let him have a look and then try again, but not to push him too much as he came into the fence for he had such a long stride he found it difficult to adjust it. "Some people choose horses with a short stride for show-jumping, but of course, a long striding gallop helps you to get across country."

At the second attempt Samson, concentrating hard, jumped the downhill fence and he jumped the uphill without a refusal, but in rather a laboured manner. Sky Pilot trotted up and down without any fuss, but Marion, who was looking quite green by the time her turn came, refused the first fence.

"Give him a short run, a longer rein and put your legs on harder," instructed the Major. "A longer rein," he shouted again, as Marion had a second refusal. After her third attempt he said, "The trouble is that *you* don't really want to go over; we'll let someone else try."

"I'll do it," said Christopher promptly.

Christopher scrambled up quickly. "These stirrups'll do," he said, and turning Crusoe he rammed him at the fence. Crusoe refused. Christopher hit him and he jumped.

"Yes," said the Major, when he returned, "but that isn't how I want to see it done. I want to see you sitting quietly and the horse jumping willingly—you're too inclined to resort to force."

"Well, at least I got him over."

"Well, now you can do it properly," the Major told him, "and keep that whip quiet. There are occasions when a horse should be punished for refusing, but this isn't one of them. It was his rider's fault, and why hit a horse for his rider's mistakes? Trot a circle, get him going well and then you won't need to. Hitting a horse won't make him enjoy jumping and there's no fun in jumping a horse that doesn't enjoy it."

At his second attempt Christopher sat more quietly but he couldn't resist kicking Crusoe on the take-off and using his outside heel whenever he thought that the Major couldn't see. Then Marion mounted and she rode at the first fence with many misgivings, but she put her legs on, held the mane and gave him a loose rein as the Major had told her, and Crusoe jumped well.

"Right," said the Major. "Now we'll just have one jump over the quarry. Trot those horses round on a large circle; get them going again.

"Now there's nothing difficult about the quarry taken this way," he went on, when the horses were going freely. "Keep up your impulsion. Give with your hands as you go up the bank and give again at the top, sit still and let your horses carry you over."

Much to their surprise, not one of the Pony Club members refused at the quarry. Truant was rather horrified to find a fence waiting for him at the top of the bank, but he collected his wits quickly and jumped it easily. Samson lost his impulsion coming up the bank and lurched over the fence in an ungraceful manner. Marion held the mane and left everything to Crusoe who jumped the log and the fence most efficiently.

"Good. Now for some lunch," said the Major.

The Pony Club members began to ride or lead their horses back to the stables. Christopher walked beside Noel.

"We *must* have some more jumps," he said. "I know it was good fun jumping them this morning, even if they were low, but we've done it now. We want some bigger ones for to-morrow."

"I don't," said Noel. "These are quite big enough for me and Truant."

"Well, he's only a youngster, but even so he's jumped everything to-day; he's ready to go a bit farther now."

John said, "You can't expect the Major to take his men off the farm work every day just to build jumps for us."

"I'd stay and do it myself," answered Christopher, "only I've arranged to play tennis again this afternoon."

CHAPTER NINE

THURSDAY, the day of the Crowley Horse Show, began badly. When the Major appeared at two minutes to ten the Pony Club members were still in the yard, tightening their girths, searching for their lost whips and arguing whose fault it was that the grooming tools were either mixed up or mislaid.

"How do you expect those horses to improve when you stand here gossiping instead of riding round and loosening them up?" demanded the Major angrily.

Noel said, "Sorry." Susan, stifling a giggle, fled in the direction of the school. Christopher began, "*I've* been here hours, only there didn't seem much point—" but the Major had marched off.

"Oh dear," said Noel, "our trots will have to be terribly active this morning."

"I vote we keep out of the way until it's blown over," Gay said to Margaret and James.

"*I'm* not afraid of old Georgie," answered Margaret, but she agreed to climb trees in the park. They had climbed half-way up one of the easier oaks when they began to feel that they might be missing something and, descending so rapidly that a large piece of James's shorts were left behind, they hurried to the school.

The riders were making turns on the forehand and the Major still seemed in a ferocious mood.

"Five years," he was saying angrily, "and every holiday we've practised turns on the forehand and you still don't know the aids."

"Oh gosh, someone's catching it. We'd better keep out of sight," said Gay.

"Oh, who cares?" said Margaret contemptuously. But

she stayed with Gay and James who kept out of sight until they saw that the schooling was over and that the Major was looking round for someone to help him with the Cavalletti.

"Just trot over these two or three times," he told the riders, when the Cavalletti were ready, "and then I've got a nice little course for you, out there in the field."

The faces of the riders brightened considerably when they heard this and they stood in their stirrups to see if the course was visible from the school.

Christopher was disappointed when at last the Major led the way to the field. Any of them can jump this, he thought, it's tiny. But John and Noel, who were both feeling worried about their young horses, were relieved.

"It looks lovely," said Noel. And Susan said, "Oh goodness, it's a figure of eight—I shall get lost."

"The rustic rails are the first fence," the Major explained. "The brush is number two, the parallels number three. Turn left and jump the stile, left again, fence five is the wattles, fence six the triple, the chicken coops are seven, turn right and the last fence is the pole over the stuffed sacks. We won't begin by jumping the whole course, because you'll work yourselves up and start interfering with your horses. Henry, I want you to jump the first three fences from a trot and then come back here. As he jumps the parallels the next person will start, but not from a standstill; he will have prepared his horse by riding on the circle. Is that clear?"

Everyone muttered that it was and Henry began to ride at what he hoped was an active trot.

"Remember to sit still," said the Major, as he started.

Echo jumped all three fences calmly. Truant wasn't as confident as Echo, but he cleared them all jumping carefully. Samson, thinking how nice it would have been to go on standing with the other horses, hit the rustic. However, the poles were heavy and he hit them hard so he was extremely careful to clear the other two fences.

"That was your fault," the Major told John. "You

116

should have insisted on his attention while you were riding on the circle."

Tranquil cleared the first two fences but, by the time he came to the parallels, he had lost his impulsion and knocked them down with his hind legs. Crusoe jumped with great flourish, but was obviously out of control.

"Try to keep him at a trot," said the Major.

Evelyn resorted to her old sharpening-up tactics instead of trying to put Quaker on the bit, and she was very busy with her hands and legs on the approach.

"No," shouted the Major. "You must sit still."

Hilary sat still, and Sky Pilot jumped with pricked ears and a wise expression; Susan cantered; Christopher rode at his collected trot and William hit the parallel bars.

"This time we'll jump the first six fences," said Major Holbrooke, "that is, everything except the chicken coops and the sacks. At the trot and do sit still. Let the horses make mistakes; they'll profit from them."

Echo hit the stile and the Major told Henry that it was his fault, because, feeling Echo's cadence quickening, he had pulled at him, causing his head to come up and his back to stiffen. "Try to keep the cadence more with your weight and with your brains than the reins," he said. "If you had relaxed them instead of pulling you might have had the desired effect."

Truant didn't like the stile because it was narrow; he made an enormous jump over it. Noel shot out of her saddle and the Major roared at her to keep still.

Tranquil refused the stile and hit the triple and the Major gave Dick another lecture on keeping his legs against the horse. "You allow your knees to stiffen over every fence; that takes your legs off and then you've no impulsion when you come to the next fence."

Philippa was out of control again. She jumped the first three fences, swept by the stile and cantered off across the field.

"Come back," roared the Major.

Christopher said, "I can't think why she was ever
117

allowed on the course. She holds us all up."

Henry grinned. "I can remember a course the Major gave two years ago," he said. "There was a boy called Christopher on it and he held everything up; he simply couldn't control his pony at all. In fact, one day we had to abandon the whole lesson and pursue the wretched pony round the countryside; Noel galloped above five miles before she managed to catch it."

Christopher turned red and then he blushed again and turned redder still. "That was quite different," he said defensively. "Fireworks was an old devil. He'd been ruined before I had him. Anyone could stop Crusoe."

The Major was lecturing Philippa.

"But he *won't* trot," she said when he paused for breath.

"Oh yes he will," contradicted the Major. "Begin again jumping. If the horse is going properly, jumping will be easy. There. Now who says that this horse won't trot?"

The experienced horses—Quaker, Sky Pilot, Wonder and William—jumped the little fences easily.

"Now just the last four fences," said the Major. "Put your legs on a little harder for the last two, but don't start tipping about and disturbing the horses."

All the horses were suspicious of the chicken coops and the stuffed sacks, but none refused. After approaching cautiously, they jumped with care and much higher than was necessary.

"Good," said the Major. "Now we'll do some cross-country."

Henry ran for the Land-Rover and the other riders started off across the fields.

"Gosh, there's a difference in Samson," John told Noel. "Does he look different? He feels a hundred per cent better."

"He looks miles better, much better balanced and he goes more freely than he used to. I think that all the young horses have improved."

The Land-Rover reached the Little Heath field at the same moment as the riders. Henry mounted and the

118

Major gave each of the spectators a flag and sent them to mark the course.

"Keep outside all the flags," he told the riders. "They're designed to give you the right approach. I don't want you cutting your corners yet—that comes with experience. This flag is the start and the finish; jump the rails and ditch, the downhill fence, outside the valley flag, jump the uphill fence and finish with the quarry. Ride at a trot and when the first person is over the downhill fence the next person may start, and so on."

The horses and riders were confident. Only Philippa had any fears and Crusoe had enough confidence for two.

"Good," said the Major, as one by one the riders returned, "this is much better; everyone has improved. Now at the canter, Henry."

In turn, the riders cantered away. Leaning forward with their weight in the stirrups, they cantered easily, not pushing or pulling, but contentedly one with their mounts. Crusoe was out of control down the hill, but Philippa managed to turn him round the flag at the bottom, the uphill steadied him and she finished quietly. Evelyn didn't try to show off; she kept her cadence down the hill. Hilary and Susan were enjoying themselves, but Christopher felt cheated. Everyone could canter downhill now, he thought, so there was no more fun in it. Why couldn't the Major find something more difficult for them to do? He wanted to show—to prove—that he was the best.

"There's just one more thing for to-day," said the Major, when everyone had completed the course at the canter, "the quarry the other way round."

"Now the fun begins," said Henry.

"Goodness, I'm bound to fall off," shrieked Susan.

Noel hoped gloomily that Truant had a head for heights, and Philippa said that she couldn't possibly do it. It was much too difficult for her and she thought she had better stand on one side.

Henry told Philippa, that there was no such word as can't, and Noel told Henry that he was unbearably smug.

119

"When you've quite finished making your last wills and testaments," said the Major, "perhaps we could begin? Just trot at it, Henry, but get your horse going first. There's no difficulty about this at all provided you take it slowly and keep forward down the slope."

The morale of the riders rose when Henry and Echo jumped the fence and rode down the bank with ease. Truant followed with more caution but equal ease. It was Samson who had no head for heights; he jumped the fence but, when he saw the quarry yawning before him, he dithered for several moments before John persuaded him to venture down. Tranquil lost his impulsion, but the jumps were so small that it didn't matter. The Major threatened Philippa with horrid consequences if she went out of a trot and made her take a very short run indeed. Once she was over, the quarry seemed to lose its terrors, and the remaining riders jumped it with abandon.

The Major told Evelyn that she had ridden too fast; her horse must learn to jump slowly before he jumped fast, then he would always come back to hand without fighting or pulling. He told Christopher that he had been too busy with his reins and that had caused William to jump flat, and Susan that she had tipped forward down the bank. Then he said, "Well, that's enough for to-day. If anyone has any time or energy to spare this afternoon we shall be very glad of some labour; I want to fix up two or three more fences."

"Oh good," said Christopher. "I'll stay, but can I telephone my mother?"

"Certainly," answered the Major. "Come round to the house when you've put your pony away."

Henry dismounted. "My legs feel most odd," he said. "Do you reckon we're improving, Uncle George?" he asked when he had driven out of earshot of the members.

"Do you reckon you are? That's much more important," answered the Major.

"W—ell, yes. I must say I feel *quite* different—much more at home somehow—and Echo's far less bolshy."

"What about the others?"

"Noel says Truant's a different horse. But I don't know about the others, except for John; he sings a perpetual hymn of praise about you and Samson, yet before the course he was in deeper despair than anyone."

"Well, if I've three satisfied clients, I can't call my time wasted," said the Major.

"I thought we'd have a competition on Saturday," he went on, "it'll be interesting to see what happens."

"Is that official? It'll throw some of our friends into confusion and others into an orgy of competitive spirit."

"You can tell them if you like," said the Major. "It'll be a One Day Event. Dressage and show-jumping in the morning and cross-country after lunch. And if their parents want to watch they can come."

"What a treat. I'm glad so many miles separate me from my fond family," said Henry, bringing the Land-Rover to a halt before the house. "I'll run and spread the glad news before lunch."

He met Christopher hurrying in to telephone. "Good news for you, Christopher," he said. "More laurels to be won and honours gained—my esteemed uncle announces a One Day Event on Saturday."

"Really? How simply super. Good old Major. The whole week will have been worth while after all. Are we going to have some decent fences?"

"Ask the boss. But you'd better be tactful about his fences or you may get slung out on your ear."

Christopher laughed. "The Major doesn't mind what I say," he answered, "we're good friends."

Noel had already left for home, but Henry amused himself by horrifying John, Philippa and Susan with exaggerated accounts of the One Day Event.

"This reminds me of building the wall around the House of Stone," said Henry, shovelling earth. "Do you remember in *Four Feathers*? I feel that we're sealing our own doom too."

121

"Yes, it was gruesome. Mason's terribly good at being gruesome. Last summer, while I was staying with you, I read the one in which they put people in nets and drown them under motor boats," said Noel.

"Hallo, how are you two getting on?" asked Christopher, coming up behind them.

"We're quite happy with our mud pies."

"I don't see how we're going to bank this properly," said Christopher, kicking at the loose earth which Noel and Henry had been shovelling against the old boundary bank into Little Heath copse. "The first horse'll get over if it's lucky, but by the time I get there the whole thing will have collapsed. John and Jeffrys are scratching out a sort of hollow, which the Major calls the water, but even if he gets the water there it'll have soaked away by Saturday, and the others were told to raise all those little rails, but nothing's to be over three feet."

"Well, go and occupy yourself usefully; make some better jumps since you don't like any of ours. There are six posts and four rails in the Land-Rover. Not to mention a beetle for bashing and a hammer and nails. Uncle George wants a right-angle fence, but you'd better ask him for location and measurements before you begin."

"Oh, O.K.," said Christopher ungraciously. When he had gone, Noel kicked the bank and asked, "How *is* the Major going to make it solid?"

"He has a method," answered Henry, "it's done with a giant crochet-hook, railway sleepers and cable wire, but you need a bit of a bank to build against if you want it firm enough to jump next day; that's why it has to be in this unsalubrious spot with trees all round for us to knock our heads on."

"Oh dear," said Noel, leaning on her spade, "I do wish that we weren't having a competition. It was all so nice and peaceful before—"

"And now you've got the needle," said Henry, forestalling her.

CHAPTER TEN

HENRY was distracted. "We're never going to be ready by ten o'clock," he said, grabbing the hose and dragging it in tangled confusion to the Land-Rover.

"Hallo, you seem in slight difficulty," Dick observed.

"Yes, blast the thing; help me 'eave it in, will you? Uncle George has suddenly become ambitious about to-morrow, he's been ringing up all his friends and inviting them over and now I suppose he wants to give them a show. Talk about throwing Christians to the lions. Are you busy?"

"No," answered Dick.

Henry produced a copy of a Pony Club Test from his pocket. "Could you organise a few dressage markers in appropriate spots?" he asked. "Uncle G. says half the school is more or less the right size. Use the half farthest from the gate and put the judges at the eastern end so they won't have to look into the sun."

"I'll do my best. Has it got to be very accurate?"

"No, if Uncle G. doesn't approve he can sort it out before to-morrow."

Everyone was in the yard, except Henry and the elder Radcliffes, when the Major came out to distribute copies of the dressage test. "There's nothing to it," he replied to the cries of horror which greeted him. "It doesn't need learning—the wretched ponies all know it by heart when they have done it twice."

"Do you hear that, Wonder?" asked Susan, with a giggle. "It's just as much your fault as mine if we go wrong."

"I don't think I want to ride in it," said Marion. "You ride, Philippa. It's your turn really."

Henry, Hilary and Evelyn arrived in the yard at the same moment. Henry was still harassed. "It's two minutes to ten; for heaven's sake get up, everyone," he said. "We all ought to be riding our horses in."

When everyone was in the school the Major explained that there would not be time to go through all three phases of the One Day Event that morning.

"We've practised all the necessary movements for the dressage test during the last four days," he said, "and, as this is primarily a cross-country course, I'm going to leave you to practise the test on your own. I shall see you round the show-jumping course and then go up to Little Heath, where we shall practise over the new fences. While one person is riding round the show-jumping course, another will be practising in the dressage arena and two others will be preparing their horses; one for show-jumping and one for dressage. When anyone has completed the show-jumping and dressage they will go up to Little Heath and rest their horse until I come."

"There's going to be chaos," Henry observed cheerfully, and Christopher said: "I think it's a simply super idea. We shall be able to get our horses going properly."

The Major watched the Pony Club members riding their horses in and he gave a lot of good advice and, here and there, a word of praise. He told Noel that her elbows were much less stiff, that she wasn't looking down so much, but that she still didn't sit into her horse enough. She should try to lengthen her legs and lower her heels. He asked John if Samson felt as different as he looked, but he told him that he was still using his hands too much in a hopeless attempt to pull him together, whereas it was only by driving Samson's long hind legs under his body that he could be shortened and made lighter in hand. He told June to feel her horse with her legs *all* the time; Evelyn to drop her knee a little lower. He said that Dick was idle.

Then it was time to begin. "Who would like to jump first?" asked the Major. John said that he wouldn't mind. Christopher said that he wanted to get William going *properly* before *he* began, and Noel muttered that she might as well go early and get it over.

Noel and John disappeared to the field; Henry asked the remaining riders, "Who wants first bash at dressage?"

"Oh, I'll start the ball rolling," answered Dick, "inactive horse, stiff knees and all."

Henry grinned. "I'll follow you then," he said.

Evelyn asked, "What about me?"

"O.K., said Dick, "you can go first if you like."

Samson jumped the show-jumping course only knocking the gate, which pleased John for every fence · had been raised three inches and now stood at three feet.

Truant jumped a clear round slowly and with great caution. Only Susan was waiting to jump next so John and Noel returned to the school and told Evelyn and Dick that they were wanted.

Henry entered the arena next, calling to Noel to watch him. Hilary, deciding that the dressage queue was too long, announced that she was going to jump. Noel thought that Echo was going far better than he had at the Mantwick tests and, when Henry finished, she told him so. "You make it look easy now," she said.

"Oh good, that is a compliment indeed," said Henry, patting Echo. "Now, shall I look at you?"

"No, I've bagged next," shouted Christopher, "but you can look at me if you like."

Christopher couldn't get William going to his liking. He went over the same movements again and again, he became rather cross and then he dismounted and tightened the drop noseband. "There, now you'll have to drop your nose," he told William.

Henry raised his eyebrows and Noel asked, "Are you going to be *much* longer, Christopher?"

"Yes, come on. Buck up," added John. "You're making a bottleneck and we shall have the Major swearing."

"Well, he wants us to do it properly, doesn't he?" asked Christopher aggressively.

"You're not the only pebble on the beach," said June, riding away towards the show-jumping course.

And John said, "She's quite right; after all, we've all got

to have a go before lunch and the cross-country's supposed to be more important."

"The cross-country is too jolly easy."

"You've got a swelled head, that's your trouble."

Christopher reddened. "It's easy to say that," he replied. "But you know jolly well that I can jump higher and just because some of you can't we have to have these beastly little fences that one can hardly see."

"They're all three feet," began John, but Noel wailed: "Oh, do stop arguing with him, John, you're making him slower than ever."

"Much better," the Major was shouting. "*Much* better," and though Glory refused once or twice, it seemed to Henry that she was enjoying herself much more than he had ever seen her before.

Echo jumped well, very fast and free, but he hit the stile.

"Did you feel how he lost his cadence then?" asked the Major afterwards. "He stiffened and jumped flat."

"Yes, I felt it all right," answered Henry, "but what does one do to prevent it?"

"It is usually the rider who causes it; somehow one disturbs the horse. You thought, 'lord, here's the stile; we're going too fast,' and you disturbed Echo by pulling on the reins. I think if you had trusted him he was coming right and would have cleared it; but try again. This time leave him alone and we'll see what happens."

Echo cleared the stile.

"They say that to sit still and do nothing is the most difficult thing of all," observed the Major. "No one else seems to want to jump," he went on, looking round the deserted field.

"I'll go and hustle them up. There's a queue for the arena and they're all afraid of losing their places."

Henry found Christopher still occupying the arena. Noel was looking even more dreary and John was obviously working himself into a rage.

"Who hasn't jumped?" Henry asked Dick.

126

"Christopher," he answered, "and what about Marion?"

Henry rode towards Marion, who was practising in a corner of the school. "Go and jump," he roared at her. "Hurry. Uncle George is becoming enraged."

"You are a beast," said Noel, as Marion fled. "Now she'll be so flustered she won't be able to do a thing."

Henry grinned. "Don't judge others by yourself," he said. "The Hunters are inspired by bullying."

"Well, go and bully Christopher," said Noel. "He's being an absolute beast."

Henry removed Christopher by shouting, "Uncle George says that if you don't go at once you can't jump."

Christopher rode away unwillingly. Noel trotted a circle and then began her test. It was a tidy-looking test but, to Henry, Truant seemed rather stiff and apprehensive. John followed Noel and he asked Henry and Noel to watch him. Except for carrying out all the movements just past, instead of at the markers, they thought it looked good.

"I felt as though I were pushing a car in gear. My legs!" complained John.

"He didn't look like that. He looked very handsome."

"We'd better go and cross-country, before Uncle George blows up," said Henry.

Susan shrieked, "Oh goodness, it's my turn now. Noel, you *must* watch me."

Noel stayed to watch Susan; Henry gave Echo to Hilary and ran to fetch the Land-Rover. Marion came riding back from her jumping. "He's going much better," she told June and Hilary. "Oh dear, I do think Philippa's the limit, she's gone to play tennis instead of watching; she's sure to let him down to-morrow."

When Susan had finished her test, she and Noel rode over to Little Heath leading Echo and leaving Hilary and June to instruct Marion who had never ridden a test.

"At the markers, not a mile afterwards," they could hear June saying as they rode away. "Oh, Marion, you are a fool; look, like this," and then they heard Hilary, who had evidently remembered the Major's words, add: "All movements are carried out when the rider's shoulders are level with the appropriate marker."

They found the Major and the other Pony Club members by the right angle fence. Dick and Tranquil had just refused the second fence.

"All right, don't upset him," said the Major. "He's never seen a fence like it before. Let him have a look and then go back and try again."

Tranquil jumped both fences at his second attempt and then it was Christopher's turn. He took the first fence straight and then swung William round and jumped the second one.

"You see what I mean about taking the first fence at an angle," said the Major, turning to the other members. "If you take it at a slant you are already right for the second fence. The horse is confronted by his problem and can estimate his stride; you don't lose any ground or speed, which, as you saw, Christopher did. Right, Henry; see if you can take it at the correct angle."

Henry cantered a circle.

"One thing about William, he is handy," Christopher told Noel and Susan.

Henry rode at the fences and suddenly Echo realised what he had to do, jumped the first fence on a slant and continued without hesitation over the second.

John and Evelyn had already jumped so Noel followed Henry. "Put the legs on," the Major told her. "If your horse is on the bit he will go straight and there will be no need to lose impulsion by pulling on the reins."

Truant jumped at the correct angle, but not with the same flourish as Echo.

The Major looked at his watch. "We'd better get on," he said. "The bank is next."

"Oh goodness," said Susan. "I'm sure I can't do it. I've never jumped a bank before, have you, Noel?"

"No, never. I expect I shall fall off," answered Noel.

"It's just like any other fence," said the Major. "Take it

128

quietly, sit still and remember to 'give' twice. It's two jumps, you see—one up and one down. If you stay with your horse you'll be all right. First of all just trot them over the ordinary bank into the wood and then we'll jump the made-up one out into the field."

Most of the horses and ponies were accustomed to scrambling over the little boundary banks out hunting so they made no difficulty about going into the wood. Only Truant thought it worthy of a real jump.

Evelyn was in the lead; she rode at the big bank, which was about three feet high and faced with railway sleepers, in a rough but determined manner. Quaker jumped up and Evelyn was left behind. The Major roared something about legs and Quaker jumped down, leaving Evelyn in the air, but she caught up with him, landing with a loud thud in the saddle.

"Very bad," said the Major. "You weren't in your stirrups during the approach so you were left behind when he took off and you never caught up again. You must *not* sit in the back of your saddle."

John and Samson weren't much better. They reached the top of the bank successfully, but there Samson's nerve failed him and he stood dithering at the edge, a horrified expression on his face.

"Keep your legs on," yelled the Major, and at last Samson summoned the courage to jump down.

Christopher refused twice and he was beginning to get angry with William when the Major said, "It's your fault, you're holding him on too tight a rein."

"He'll run out," answered Christopher, but when, with his reins hanging in exaggerated loops, he rode at the bank again, William jumped it without any fuss.

Dick and Tranquil had one refusal and then scrambled up and down in a series of lurches.

Noel had come to the conclusion that banks were much more difficult than the Major had made out when Henry and Echo jumped it magnificently and raised everyone's morale.

E

Truant was obviously filled with misgivings, but he jumped up from a standstill and down after he had looked over the edge to make sure that it was safe. Noel held on to the mane.

The Major cursed Susan again for riding at a fence from a standstill with her horse off the bit. "Of course that mare refuses," he said, "and it's entirely your fault."

"Sorry," said Susan, patting Wonder and trotting back up the track for a second attempt.

"Right. Now you can each have another turn," said the Major. "And do use your brains this time. Don't keep on and on making the same silly mistakes."

Except for Echo, they all jumped the bank much better the second time, and then the Major hurried them towards the water jump; a shallow ditch about eight feet broad, made watertight with a tarpaulin, winged with hurdles and filled from a tap in the corner of the field.

"What a super jump," said John. Noel said, "Ugh, how can you? It looks beastly to me; I know I'm going to fall in."

"Well, one thing, it is summer," remarked Susan.

Marion gave a gasp. "*I'm* sure to fall in."

"Goody, there's going to be three of us," said Susan.

"Four," corrected John, "I'm the obvious person."

"I hope you can all swim," remarked the Major. "But seriously, there's no difficulty about water. Some horses don't like it at first, but it's just like any other obstacle—if you school over a nice small water jump the horse will soon get confidence in himself; the real trouble is that they don't see enough of it. With a young horse you want a ground line: a log or a little brush fence in front of it to show him where to take off. Later on you can dispense with it and jump your water plain, or with a rail over the middle.

"Now it's quite obvious that if your horse has got to clear a great width he mustn't take off too far away. Don't steady him as you might for a straight fence; send him on and ride with a giving rein, but don't send him on so early that he's lost his impetus by the time he reaches the water; he should be gaining speed at the moment he takes off. It's not really as complicated as it sounds and this isn't a big jump. If you sit still and give them their heads, they'll take you over."

"We hope," said John.

"And devotedly pray," added Henry. "I'm ill-advised enough to be wearing my best breeches."

The Major kicked the bundles of brushwood, that were making the ground line, a little closer to the water. Evelyn cantered a circle, increased her speed as she turned for the jump and then, three or four strides away, she hit Quaker: he refused. "Why did you do that?" demanded the Major. "You disturbed him and took his mind off the jump at a vital moment; all he *could* do was to stop."

Evelyn glowered. "He was going to refuse, I felt it."

"Well, he didn't look like it, and even if you thought he might stop that was quite the wrong moment to hit him. On the take-off if you must, but never coming up to the fence. Go on, try again, and keep *still*."

Quaker jumped at the second attempt and the Major told Henry, who was already cantering a circle, to follow on. Echo jumped the water easily and Henry rode back patting him and looking very pleased.

"That was most unexpected," he said.

"Echo looked as though he'd been jumping water for years," said Dick.

John rode with tremendous determination; but Samson refused at the last moment and slid to the edge. "Let him have a look," said the Major. "Good. Now don't ride him so hard; you pushed him out of his cadence; sit still; give him a chance to jump."

Much to everyone's surprise Samson did jump when John rode him with less determination.

"There you are," said the Major, and then, looking at Dick, "but that doesn't mean that you take the legs off. Push, but quietly, and in time with the horse's stride."

Tranquil jumped the water and so did Truant, clearing

131

it with an enormous leap, which caused Noel to lose a stirrup. Christopher and Susan both jumped it easily, though Susan took a firm hold of the mane.

"Right," said the Major. "You can each have one more jump and then I've finished with you for to-day."

This time all the horses jumped well.

"Good," said the Major. "Ride them home quietly." And turning to the late arrivals, "You see, there's nothing in it. Having accustomed our horses to jumping ditches, we can jump eight feet of water, and having jumped eight we can almost certainly jump twelve."

"Golly," said Susan, "I hope not." And Noel said, "I think the Major's a beast to belittle our achievement; I was feeling awfully pleased with myself and then he says there's nothing in it."

"I think it was *enormous*," said Henry, "and I'm frightfully proud of myself whatever Uncle George says."

"Oh, Henry, you are silly," giggled Susan.

"Well, it was quite a decent jump for a young horse," said John in serious tones.

"I agree with the Major," said Christopher aggressively. "There was nothing in it; it's hardly more than a ditch."

Evelyn, who was looking back to watch Hilary, said, "Marion Hunter's off again. Honestly, if I rode as badly as that girl does, I'd give up."

CHAPTER ELEVEN

THE sun, which had shone all through the course, was still shining on the last day, but with less vigour; there was a feeling of autumn in the air.

The yard at Folly Court was filled with horses and ponies from an early hour for, besides the competitors, Margaret, James and Gay were mounted; the Major had told them that they might bring their ponies and act as messengers in the afternoon.

So many parents, friends and hunting people had been invited to watch that the competitors had decided that it was a public occasion and were grooming their horses accordingly.

Noel had washed Truant's two white hind socks and Tranquil's one white fore sock. Henry, John, Dick and Christopher had all groomed until their arms ached. James had borrowed a tin of hoof oil and a brush from Blake and was oiling all the hoofs. June outshone everyone; she was wearing her dark blue coat and Wilson had plaited Glory's mane and tail.

Evelyn had drawn number one and she was pleased. "I don't want to hang about all day," she said, and, "I shall get round before the feeble people cut the take-offs up with their refusing."

Number two was Christopher. He'd put on a double bridle for the test, because he was determined to have William really collected.

Susan and June, who were riding third and fourth, were telling each other all the frightful things they were going to do. Susan was giggling, but June said, "It's all very well for you, but Mummy'll be furious."

Noel felt faintly sick and her legs were weak with the needle. Truant wasn't going forward properly and she was steering with the reins. He's too fresh, she thought drearily, as he shied at imaginary evil in the hedge.

Henry, whose number was seven, had only just brought Echo out. He had reckoned that he wouldn't be wanted before half-past ten, so he was riding quietly and checking his seat. Heels down. Am I tall above the saddle and tall below? Is Echo in front of the legs?

Captain Julian Barton, the well-known rider and judge, who was an old friend of the Major's arrived at one minute to ten and was hurried straight to his table, where Mrs. Holbrooke was waiting to write down the marks. Henry rode in pursuit of Evelyn. "They're all set now," he said. "Are you ready?"

"I've been ready for hours. I don't find it necessary to ride round counting my horse's legs with a grim expression like the rest of you."

"You're lucky," answered Henry. "Would you like to go and walk round outside the arena? Captain Barton will ring the bell when he wants you to begin."

Evelyn gave an impatient snort. "The fuss you're all making!"

The bell rang directly Evelyn appeared. She swung Quaker round, entered the arena at A. At X she halted and gave a hasty bow.

Hilary was the only competitor who watched Evelyn's test; the others were all too busy riding their own horses. Hilary thought, oh damn. She's making a muck of it. I know she doesn't really care, but why enter? It's beastly for the rest of us. She looked across the arena at James and Margaret, who were also watching. Perhaps they don't notice, she thought hopefully.

Christopher was confident. He watched the tail-end of Evelyn's test with a slightly superior smile. The others mightn't be quite so bad, he thought, but most of them would make a hopeless mess of it. The poor old Major simply wasted his time on them.

"How's William this morning?" asked Miss Sinclair on her way to collect Evelyn's marks.

134

"Oh, going very well, thank you."

Evelyn left the arena. The bell rang. Calmly and with deliberation, Christopher entered at A.

Mrs. Cresswell watched Christopher ride his test and, as she watched, her panic grew. She felt certain that June couldn't carry out the movements as neatly as this. She'll be beaten easily, she thought. Why did I encourage her to take up dressage? Why didn't I advise her to stick to showing? We shall look such fools if she's beaten by all and sundry. Mrs. Cresswell left the school and hastened across the show-jumping field. June pretended to be engrossed in her schooling and ignored her mother's beckoning signals.

"June, dear," said Mrs. Cresswell, when at length she reached her, "do try to drive Glory together. She looks so long and sloppy compared with that Minton boy's pony. *And* he's wearing a double bridle. It hardly seems right when the Major forbade you to do so. What's right for one is right for another, and of course you can get an animal more collected in a double; it's most unfair."

"Oh Mummy, don't be such a fool," answered June. "Everyone knows that too early use of the double bridle spoils the development of the horse's cadence and paces. Christopher's just getting his horse from the front instead of engaging its quarters. If he likes to be a fool, I don't care. The Major's told him to ride in a snaffle, but he thinks he knows everything. I'm not going to spoil the development of Glory's paces just for one silly test."

"Well really! Is that true, June? You certainly seem to have learned a great deal in a very short time."

June said, "Susan's going now; I'm next. I'm going to trot a circle and make sure that Glory's in front of the legs and on the bit."

Finding herself ignored, Mrs. Cresswell hurried back to the arena.

Susan said, "Well done, Christopher. That looked awfully good. Wonder's off the bit; I'm going to do a
135

simply terrible test; I nearly went home for a double bridle too."

"You might have thought of that before."

Mrs. Cresswell joined Mrs. Radcliffe. "I think that Minton boy had his pony rather cramped in that double bridle, don't you?" she said. "It's quarters didn't seem as well engaged as they might have been. June's new to this, you know. She's never done dressage before this week, but she's taking to it very well and she won't hear of riding Glory in a double bridle until her paces have leveloped."

"Oh good," said Mrs. Radcliffe. "Now do explain it to me. I've come to watch because this wretched dressage has divided my children into two camps and neither I nor my husband can understand what it's all about."

"The important thing," said Mrs. Cresswell firmly, "is to be on the bit."

Susan's test was pleasant, but rather inaccurate. She shrieked to June as she rode out, "Did you see my *turns*? They were terrible!"

"You are a fool; why didn't you keep the legs on?" demanded June.

Mrs. Cresswell twisted her hands together in an agony of suspense all through June's test. She could not tell how good or how bad it was, but she felt almost certain that Christopher's neatness and accuracy had her beaten.

The Major was wandering about, trying to look busy, for he had no wish to be buttonholed by anxious parents, but really watching the dressage with all his attention.

"Oh, Henry, do get your uncle away before I begin," wailed Noel. "He does put me off so and Truant's going terribly badly. My stirrups seem to get longer every minute and my reins get shorter."

"He's pretending that he doesn't know any of us this morning. You'll be all right; put the legs on."

"How can I? They're weak with the needle."

Christopher rushed up. "Evelyn's marks are out," he said. "Miss Sinclair's adding up. Minus 68."

"Under half marks," said Henry. "In an International Competition she wouldn't be allowed to go on."

"Hilary's going in. Oh, I do feel awful," moaned Noel.

"For heaven's sake, shut up," said Christopher irritably. "Anyone would think it was your first show."

Hilary's test was quiet and accurate. She made no large blunders and Christopher, watching critically, decided that she would be close enough to him to be a serious rival in the show-jumping and cross-country.

"I'm going to watch Noel," said Susan, "and then I'm going to put Wonder away until the jumping."

Noel was looking at the ground before she ever entered the area, and as she rode up the centre she was conscious of Truant's wavering hoofs.

Oh dear, she thought, as she halted at X, that wasn't square. He's not on the bit, she thought, holding him in to the corners with her outside rein and desperately flapping her inside leg.

"How's she done?" asked Henry, riding up as his turn approached.

"Oh, she's boshed it up good and proper," answered Christopher. "Even took the wrong course; as if anyone *could* forget a Pony Club test."

"Don't be beastly. Truant's jolly difficult to ride," protested Susan.

"Well, whose fault is that? She broke him in."

"Actually, she hasn't done too badly," Hilary told Henry, "but not as well as I expected."

"I shan't be the only one to forget the test *this* time," observed John. "Good luck, Henry," he added. "I follow you so I'd better go and have another ride round."

" 'Say not the struggle naught availeth,' " quoted Henry, as a miserable-looking Noel rode by him.

"I was terrible," she answered, patting Truant half-heartedly. She escaped from a group of commiserating members and rode back to the stables. She put Truant away and, leaning against his door, thought how hopeless she had been and how all her hopes were dashed. Then

137

she began to wonder how Henry had fared and she remembered that she had never even wished him good luck. She was missing John's test too and Dick and Tranquil.

As she ran back she met Henry leading Echo in.

"How did you do?"

"Not too badly. At least everyone seemed to think that it looked O.K. and it certainly felt better than that horrible performance I gave at Mantwick."

"Oh good. I am glad," said Noel. "I must go and see John and Dick; I haven't watched a single person yet."

"Nor have I. I'll join you in a minute."

"Noel, he did a simply super test," said Gay, rushing to meet her as she entered the school. "Honestly, it was miles the best, wasn't it, James?"

"Yes, miles and miles I should think."

"And he was wizardly accurate," added Gay.

"How's John been doing?" asked Noel.

"Oh, quite well. Not as good as Henry, but better than lots of people. He went on the right leg."

Noel sighed. "I shall be last," she said gloomily.

"Oh no you won't," Susan told her, and then in a whisper she added: "Evelyn was much worse."

John rode out of the arena looking hot, but happy.

"Gosh, I'm worn out," he said, "but he's quite easy once you get him going."

"Jolly good," Susan told him, and "Good luck," she called to Marion.

"Noel, come and give Tranquil and me some last minute advice," said Dick. "We've got to be a credit to your breaking."

"Don't worry, you can't be worse than me."

"Hasn't Henry told you that Mrs. Exeter's here?"

"No. Where?" asked Noel in tones of horror. "How did she know this was happening? Don't say she saw *my* dressage. Oh dear, why didn't Henry tell me?"

"I expect he knew you'd fly off the handle," answered Dick. "Look, you'd better take some interest in Tranquil; I'm going to ride in two minutes."

Noel watched Dick trotting on a circle. Tranquil really went quite well, she thought. He'd always had a longer stride and more cadence than Truant, but he was idle.

"He's going well," she said. "The only thing I can suggest is a bit more leg; he comes off the bit occasionally, especially in the transitions."

Miss Sinclair was adding marks to the scoresheet on the blackboard at regular intervals, and each time she did so there was a wild rush to see them, but Noel kept well away; she was putting off the horrid moment for as long as possible.

Marion left the arena with a cheerful smile. "It wasn't half as bad as I expected," she told Susan.

"You were jolly good," Susan answered. "Especially as it was your first time."

Dick, walking round outside the arena and waiting for the bell, decided that he didn't feel particularly nervous. Of course I don't expect to win, he thought. If I'm halfway down the list at the end of the day I'll be quite content.

The Major was moving among the members.

"First people in the jumping get ready, please," he said. "We don't want a long wait. Go on. Fetch your horses. You'll be riding in the same order."

"Did we disgrace you in the dressage?" asked Christopher.

"No, I don't think so. That is yet to come. John, you rode a very nice test."

"Henry's was good too, wasn't it?" asked Gay.

"Yes, what I saw of it, but of course one doesn't see everything from the ringside."

"Noel was much worse than I expected," said Christopher.

"She hasn't the temperament for this sort of thing," answered the Major. "Go on, get those horses."

Christopher took one more look at the scoreboard on his way to the stables.

"I'm still top," he told Susan, when he caught up with

her, "but I wish that Sinclair woman would buck up with Henry's marks. Noel's three worse than you and Hilary—minus. 53. That means she's fourth at the moment and June fifth."

"I should think John, Henry and Dick will all be better than me," said Susan.

"Who cares about the dressage?" asked Evelyn. "It's much more fun to give the dressage drips a smack in the face by making it up in the cross-country."

When at last all the marks were out it was found that Henry was leading with a minus of 36, ten marks better than his nearest rival—Christopher. John, with a minus of 48, had come into third place. Hilary and Susan stood fourth, Noel sixth, Dick was only two marks behind Noel and June only one mark behind Dick. Marion, much to her surprise, wasn't last; she was three marks better than Evelyn, with a minus of 65.

"The Major says you can't help it," Susan told Noel, when she found her gazing disconsolately at the marks, "he says that you've got the wrong temperament for this sort of thing—Christopher asked him."

"Wrong temperament himself," said Noel furiously. "And why doesn't Christopher mind his own business?"

"But people can't help their temperaments," said Susan soothingly.

"Who's throwing attacks of temperament now?" asked Henry, joining them.

"It's your foul uncle. He says I haven't got the temperament for one day events," said Noel indignantly.

"Tell him to shut his trap," suggested Henry flippantly. "You haven't done too badly, Noel. You're in what might be described as a strong challenging position."

"Sixth," muttered Noel indignantly.

"I want to watch a few people round the show-jumping. Uncle George has laid it out very craftily and it strikes me the time allowed is a trifle sharpish."

"I'd better get Truant and watch too. I seem to be in the sort of mood when I take the wrong course."

Everyone had left the school for the show-jumping field when John rode up to look at the score. "Gosh!" he said, when he saw where he stood, "Gosh!" and he rode away looking very pleased and patting Samson.

Evelyn galloped out of the show-jumping ring cursing. "It's a stinking course," she told the people waiting to go in "The combination fences are much too close together and the whole thing's so beastly twisty. It's not funny, half the fences aren't even opposite each other."

"Oh lawkes," said Christopher.

"It'll suit you all right," Evelyn told him bitterly. "It's designed for a fourteen-hand pony."

None of the show-jumps were over three feet three, but they were solidly built and the layout was twisty. The course began diagonally across the ring with a brush, rustic rails and a gate. A left turn led to parallels and a right turn brought one to the wall. A second right turn took one to the far side of the ring, where straw bales with red and white poles above them made a formidable-looking double; close to it came the stile. On the other side of the ring a road closed and a triple brought you back to the parallels and then the wall, which was fence 10 as well as fence 5.

All the members hurried to the ringside to watch Christopher. He took up a firm contact and cantered in a circle. Keeping William very much together, he jumped the first three fences, but hit the parallels.

"He was going too slowly, surely?" said Dick.

Christopher cleared the wall, the double, the stile and the road closed, but still jumping very slowly he hit the triple, but cleared the parallels the second time.

"Ten jumping faults and three time faults," announced the judges after a moment's calculation.

"It *must* be a stiff time allowed," said John. "I'm going to have a practise jump."

Susan and Wonder jumped well, but they hit the gate and had a brick off the wall; they also collected one and a half time faults.

141

"Everyone seems to be getting time faults," remarked Noel.

"One ought to cut the corners, that's half the point of dressaging one's show-jumper," said Henry.

Golden Glory refused the parallels once and hit the second fence of the double and collected three time faults.

Hilary decided that it was time someone hurried up a bit and she bustled Sky Pilot round; he cleared everything except the double and there he had both fences down.

"Ten jumping faults, three-quarters of a time fault," announced the judges.

"That's what comes of hurrying," said Christopher. Noel was cantering a circle.

"Good luck," Susan called to her. "I'm going to try to get round without time faults," said Noel.

"You'll be a fool if you do," muttered Christopher.

Henry stopped riding round to watch. Noel started fast and Truant seemed to approve; he jumped the first three fences easily and with great impulsion. Noel had him turned for the parallels and he landed over the gate and she took them on the slant.

"Ass!" said Christopher, but Noel had turned for the wall and taken that at an angle too. She took the double and the stile straight, but without slackening speed.

"Good old Noel, she's doing marvellously," shrieked Susan. And when Truant cleared the road closed and the triple she began to shriek that it would be a clear round. But it wasn't. Noel cleared the parallels the second time, but a brick fell from the wall.

"*Bad* luck," shrieked Susan excitedly, "but never mind, you're much the best so far."

Noel jumped off and patted Truant frantically. "Wasn't he wonderful? Did it look fast? Did we have any time faults?" she asked. "It was my fault about the wall."

"Well done," said Henry, riding to the ring.

"Good luck," Noel called after him.

"Five jumping faults and no time faults," announced the judges.

142

Henry, emboldened by Noel's round, also decided to go round without time faults and he galloped round at speed, only hitting his usual bugbear—the stile.

"Five jumping faults and no time faults," announced the judges again.

Quite unexpectedly, Samson refused the first fence; but only once, and then he went on to jump a clear round. However, the refusal had cost him five faults and he had three time faults as well.

Marion was flapping and Dick was giving advice.

"Stop after the first three fences," he said, "or you'll never do that turn, and don't hurry."

"Keep him well together until the last three strides and then use your legs like hell," interrupted Christopher.

"Good luck," said Susan.

"Keep your head," advised Dick.

"She'd look jolly funny without it," said Margaret Radcliffe, beginning to giggle.

Marion jumped the first three fences well, but then she lost control and galloped past the parallels.

"Silly ass," said Christopher. "I don't suppose she'll get round."

"You're horrid," objected Susan. "If you ask me she's jolly good considering what a short time she's been riding."

"We didn't ask you," replied Christopher, "and anyone who was any good at all wouldn't have mucked up a horse like that. He's a first-class jumper; I wish I could get hold of him."

"I've seen you making a fool of yourself on him," said June.

"No one can put a spoiled horse right in five minutes."

While they were arguing, Marion had run out of the second fence of the double and that meant she had to go back and jump the first fence again. At the second attempt she jumped it and then she steadied Crusoe to a trot for the stile.

"That's twenty jumping faults and heaven knows how

many time faults," said Christopher in triumphant tones as an idle hoof removed a brick from the wall.

Dick rode in. He didn't try to hurry; he cantered round steadily, hitting the parallels the first time round and just tipping the stile.

"Ten jumping faults, 2¼ time faults. That is the last competitor in the show-jumping and there will now be a luncheon interval until two o'clock," announced the judges in relieved tones.

Miss Sinclair was adding hastily and the competitors gathered round the scoreboard.

Noel said, "Gosh, I've leapt into a very elevated position," when she realised that she was now standing third.

John was trying not to look too pleased, for he was now in second place, and Christopher was obviously dissatisfied with his score of minus 59—only one mark behind Noel, but 18 behind Henry. Hilary had fallen to fifth place with 60¾, and Susan was half a mark behind.

"Everything depends on the cross-country," decided Hilary, "though I don't think that anyone'll catch Henry."

"Why not?" asked Christopher. "With ten faults for a first refusal and thirty points for a fall it shouldn't be as difficult as all that."

"I think it's going to be terribly exciting this afternoon," said Susan. "We're *all* so close."

"I'm having my lunch out here," Henry told Noel.

"I don't feel like lunch—my needle's come back," complained Noel. "You know, I was so angry with the Major saying I hadn't the temperament that I didn't have the needle at all for the show-jumping."

"Well done, Uncle George," said Henry. "Shall I get him to say it to your face just before the cross-country? You'd be so enraged that you'd go round at a furious speed and collect maximum bonus marks."

"I'm seventeen marks behind. I'll never catch you unless you fall flat. John or Christopher might though."

"Oh, I'm going to ride at a tremendous speed," said Henry cheerfully. "I'm going to cut all the corners—

144

Christopher will disapprove—and I shall probably fall at the water and then he'll be able to say 'I told you so'."

"He still rides B.S.J.A. style, doesn't he?" said Noel. "He doesn't seem to have adopted the Italian canter."

"No, he disagrees with Uncle G. He won't go on at his fences. Still, I can't talk. My fast and free efforts seem to spell death to stiles."

"But it looks lovely."

"So did your performance. It was a pity about the wall."

"That was my fault."

None of the competitors ate much lunch because they decided to walk the cross-country course. It was apparent from a map displayed with the scoresheet that the Major had added several fences. The start was in the show-jumping field.

"Goodness, look at the cars," said Susan. "More and more keep coming. I don't see how they found out it was happening."

"Uncle George telephoned all his friends," Henry told her, "and I suppose the rest are fond parents."

"*And* Mrs. Exeter," said Noel indignantly.

"Have you seen her?" asked Henry. "I've forbidden her to speak to you until it's all over."

"Dick told me she was here, but I haven't seen her."

"Uncle George has asked her to lunch."

The first fence was the hedge out of the show-jumping field. It was quite low, for the Major had had a strip clipped specially.

"My esteemed uncle's gone quite mad," observed Henry. "He's taken the men off farmwork and put them on this sort of job; the wheat can rot for all he cares."

The second fence was a flight of wattles going downhill into the valley, and the third fence was a post and rails into Little Heath copse. Marion looked at them in horror. "But we've never practised this," she said in a dismayed voice.

"All the more fun," Christopher told her. The rails weren't high, but they were set just in front of the boundary bank, which made them look more difficult, and they were semi-fixed with cord.

"Ugh!" said Susan.

They climbed into the copse and made sure that the bank had not been altered in any way.

"I'm going to give William the devil of a whack here, just in case he tries anything on," said Christopher.

When they reached the quarry they found that instead of jumping out over the log on the cart track they had to turn slightly right-handed and jump a rail uphill.

There were many groans at this.

"Ugh, doesn't it look awful?" said Susan, and Marion said: "I shall have three refusals; I know I shall."

People grumbled and discussed the angle at which they were going to take the new fence until Henry suddenly exclaimed that it was twenty to two, then they hurried on. The downhill fence was as it had always been, and along the valley there was the right-angle fence, followed by the water. After this the course turned uphill; fence eleven was a hedge into the field next to the jumping field, and twelve was a hedge into the jumping field itself. The finish was close to the start.

Evelyn and Hilary were mounted first and they both looked cool and calm as they rode to the start.

"I've no ambition to be good at dressage," Evelyn was telling Hilary loudly. "Look at the marks you can gain in the cross-country. A good hunter can more than make up."

"Christopher's dressage has gone wrong. You can't go by him at the moment."

Christopher rode to the start with June and Susan.

"Henry's so jolly wild," he was telling them, "there's no timing or judgment in the way he jumps. Look at the way he rode this morning. I know he brought it off, but only by the skin of his teeth; it was the chanciest round ever."

"Glory likes the Italian canter," said June. "I used to

jump Wonder the old way, but Glory would never jump a stick until I started riding her like the Major said. Mummy nearly had a fit over the show-jumping; you wait till she sees me this afternoon. She'll never get over it. She likes the old-fashioned way—like you. I dare say it's all right for common horses, but for well bred high-couraged animals like Glory, give me the Italian canter."

"A fat lot you know about it," said Christopher angrily. "Look at the best show-jumping riders; they don't go round at a hundred miles an hour standing in their stirrups, they sit down and time their horses."

"I don't care about show-jumping. I'm going to train Glory and Splendour for one day events. Mummy'll have a fit when she hears, but I can't help that; I'm tired of showing."

The secretary of the West Barsetshire Hunt was the time-keeper, and various hunting friends of the Major had been press-ganged into service as jump judges.

"Thirty seconds to go," the starter told Evelyn.

"Good luck," said the other competitors.

Evelyn was galloping for the first hedge. Once she was over it she was out of sight of the waiting competitors until she appeared on the skyline riding for the quarry.

"She's not being very fast," said Hilary dismally.

"She's been hours in that quarry."

"I'm not going to look," said Noel. "It makes my needle worse."

"Poor Noel," mocked Henry, "such an unfortunate temperament."

Susan was pulling up her girths.

"We ought to have breastplates," said John gloomily. "I bet my saddle slips back going up that hill."

"What's it like? How did you do? Is it awful?" asked the other competitors crowding round Evelyn, as she dismounted from her blowing horse.

"It's the end," she answered, "the absolute end. The quarry's simply foul."

147

"Christopher's gone. I'm next," said Susan, pulling up her girths again.

"I kicked for all I was worth," Evelyn was telling Hilary. "It was all I could do to get him over the third try. He didn't like the fence into the wood either."

Christopher also spent a long time in the quarry.

"Do you reckon that the new fence stopped him too?" asked Henry.

"I shall be very surprised if it doesn't stop everyone at least once," answered Evelyn.

"Don't spread alarm and despondency."

"I hate that beastly jump. I'm going to refuse three times," shrieked Susan.

"Don't you dare," yelled Henry.

"Thirty seconds to go," said the starter, as Christopher came galloping in.

"That jump stinks," said Christopher indignantly. "The Major's the limit springing it on us like that."

Susan appeared, galloping for the quarry, before the spectators expected her. "She's pushing on a bit," said Dick.

"And she hasn't spent as long in the quarry as most people," he added, when she reappeared.

Mrs. Cresswell was giving June advice. "Keep her together, dear, and you'd better trot at those dreadful down-hill jumps. I don't know what can have come over the Major; it's a little short of madness; someone will break their neck before the day is out."

"Oh, Mummy, don't be such a fool," said June. "We've all jumped the quarry dozens of times and if you ride with the Italian canter you don't have to keep slowing up; that's no way to collect bonus marks."

"Now, June, dear, don't be rash. Do as I say; take those nasty downhill fences slowly."

Mrs. Cresswell found Mrs. Radcliffe.

"What *do* you think of this course?" she asked. "It looks very severe to me, but June assures me that it's all

148

in the day's work and she says that you've got to gallop on to collect bonus marks."

"I think it looks terrifying," answered Mrs. Radcliffe. "And I'm not going to watch anyone over that ghastly quarry until my own family have finished."

June started at a tremendous pace.

"Lawks! She won't keep that up long," said Christopher. "She'll fall at the quarry."

Susan was shrieking breathlessly. "It's *super*. Goodness, I'm puffed. *Wasn't* Wonder good? Did we look as though we were going fast? We felt ever so fast."

"It looked terrific."

"You must have collected some bonus marks."

"What's the quarry like?"

"Did you refuse?" asked the other competitors.

"Only once," answered Susan, loosening her girths, "and that was my fault. I began to flap. The second time she just took me over."

"There's June on the hill," said John. "She's been quick."

"I bet she sticks at the quarry," said Christopher.

Hilary was getting ready, tightening her girths and ramming on her crash cap. "I'm going to take it steady," she told her mother. "I want to jump a clear round and I'm not going to break Sky Pilot's wind for a bonus mark, besides there hasn't been a clear round yet."

June rode in patting Glory, who was hardly blowing at all. "She only stopped twice; once going into the wood and once out of the quarry. Last year she wouldn't jump a stick. Where's Mummy? I want some apples."

Hilary was on her way, pounding steadily down the hill. Noel was beginning to panic. Her girths were loose and she kept dropping her whip. Susan loaned hers, which had a loop for the wrist.

"I'm going to trot up the hill," she said. "Directly he begins to puff I'm going to trot. I shall trot in and out of the quarry too. I'm sure he's not fit enough."

"Poor Noel, she simply hasn't the temperament," said

149

Henry. "She really ought to give up competition riding."

"Hilary's doing awfully well. I'm sure she didn't refuse in the quarry—she's out already," announced Susan.

"You've got to go a fearsome lick," Henry told Noel.

"I'm sure he's not fit enough," protested Noel.

"Well, if he isn't you can always pull up."

Noel said, "Of course, no one's gone downhill fast enough. I might gain a bit there."

"That's the idea—put the legs on," said Henry.

Hilary was over the last hedge. Noel's legs felt weak. "Thirty seconds to go." How long was that, Noel wondered. She began to canter towards the start.

"Fifteen seconds to go." She was too near. She circled hastily. "Five seconds—go."

She forgot her weak legs as the heady joy of speed possessed her. She hardly noticed the first hedge. Down the hill, just as fast as on the flat; there was no need to steady him; he felt perfectly balanced.

Here was the uphill. "Take it easy," she told Truant, "there is a jump at the top." He steadied himself for the jump into the wood and, miraculously in time with his stride, came Noel's legs. Truant steadied himself again for the bank. He was jumping marvellously, full of confidence and fire, thought Noel. Now for the quarry. He steadied again. "Well done," she told him, as he landed.

"Now this is different but quite nice." Truant looked at the uphill fence, shortened his stride, popped over and galloped on. "Now the downhill fence, but you don't mind that." Truant took the right angle fence at speed; he cleared the water easily. Now, where do we go next? he seemed to ask galloping on with pricked ears.

"Only two more," Noel told him. She steadied him a little up the hill, but he was still going strongly and she felt like singing as she jumped the last hedge and galloped in.

"Well done," shouted Henry, who was under starter's orders. "Good luck," Noel shouted back.

"Did you refuse anything?" demanded the other competitors, engulfing Noel and Truant.

"No; he was terribly good," she answered, loosening Truant's girth and undoing his drop noseband.

"You went a bat!" said John.

Christopher said, "It's all very well for those big horses; we ought to be divided into two sections."

"Well, the ponies are the experienced jumpers."

"So what?" asked Christopher aggressively.

"Don't be so jolly unsporting," Hilary told him.

"Look at Henry," said Noel. "He's through the quarry already."

Echo was going well, thought Henry, and so far he had remembered his plans. He could cut off a bit here as he turned for the downhill fence and another bit if he took the right angle at an even greater angle. He took the water straight, but he had turned uphill by the time he landed. He galloped in over the last two hedges. Noel was waiting for him at the finish.

"That was wonderful, terribly fast and scientific," she said.

"Echo's not a bit puffed, he could have kept it up for another mile easily."

The competitors who had finished were discussing the placings. "Henry must have won," they said. "But Noel wast fast and clear and Hilary did well; then there's Susan, Christopher and June."

"What is the use of trying to work it out?" asked Hilary. "We shall know soon enough."

"John's going well. Samson certainly does cover the ground," remarked Henry.

Noel sat down on the grass. "It's a lovely day, not too hot," she said, noticing the weather for the first time.

Marion was collecting advice from everyone. "What's it *really* like?" she asked every few moments.

John hadn't time to think as he galloped round; jumps appeared in a seemingly endless succession. He trotted into the quarry and then sent Samson on for the out fence. He was filled with elation when they jumped it without a refusal. Now I must make up some time, he thought, and he hurried Samson a little as they turned downhill. Samson jumped the next fence rather flat and, still going at speed, came at the right angle. He jumped the first fence, came wrong at the second, hit the top rail and stumbled to his knees. John shot off over his shoulder.

"Blast," he said, jumping to his feet quickly and catching Samson. He mounted hastily and found his stirrups as he rode at the water. Samson jumped it easily and galloped on uphill to the last two fences.

At the start they were trying to raise Marion's morale. "It's a wizard course, honestly," Susan told her.

"I enjoyed it tremendously," Noel added.

"I shouldn't go too fast as it's your first effort."

John came galloping in with a red face, his bowler crooked and grass stains on his coat. As Marion disappeared downhill at a zigzagging canter, John told the other competitors about his fall. "I ought to be knocked on the head," he finished in disgruntled tones, "to go and collect thirty penalty points for a fall when Samson cleared everything."

"Still, you pushed on quite a bit," Henry consoled him. "I reckon you washed out a good many penalty points with bonus marks."

"It was all my fault. You see, I pushed him out of his cadence just like I used to; I suppose it was being excited. Still, I'm very pleased with him, I never thought he'd jump so well."

"Marion's stopped at the wood," said Christopher.

"Oh dear," wailed Susan, "I do want her to get round."

"I'm not going all out for bonus marks," Dick told Noel. "It's too much of a responsibility with someone else's horse. I'll do my best and try to get a clear round."

"O.K., said Noel, "that's what I thought I was going to do; but when you get going you can't help going fast—it's lovely."

Dick was soon on his way and Noel stayed to watch

Tranquil when the other competitors rushed to find how Marion had fared.

Tranquil jumped into the wood. Dick wasn't hurrying and he still wasn't hurrying when he left the wood and disappeared in the quarry."

"I don't believe Tranquil refused," said Noel excitedly.

John said, "I'm taking Samson in now," and Susan came to tell Noel that Marion had only had four refusals: one at the wood, two in the quarry, and one at the water. "Wasn't that good?" she asked.

"Awfully good," agreed Noel rather absent-mindedly.

Dick still wasn't hurrying when he came galloping in. "I ran out at the second part of the right-angle affair," he told Noel apologetically. "I'm afraid it was my inactive legs again."

They watered and fed their horses and then they lingered in the yard, watching them eat and recalling the wonderful way they had jumped and galloped.

"There's nothing to equal cross-country," said Henry. "It's much more fun than show-jumping."

"Yes, it goes on so much longer," agreed Noel.

"And quarries are super," said Susan.

They were still lingering when Gay came clattering into the yard on a weary-looking Biddy.

"The results are ready," she shrieked. "All competitors urgently wanted in the school, please."

Henry was reasonably certain that he had won, but all the others were in suspense; none of them knew how the bonus marks would work out; so they all tried to look as casual as possible.

The Major was sitting down having a rest and Miss Sinclair announced the results.

"First," she said, "number 7, Henry Thornton, with twenty-one-and-a-half penalty points.

"Second, number 6, Noel Kettering, with minus 42.

"Third, number 5, Hilary Radcliffe, minus $54\frac{3}{4}$.

"Fourth, number 3, Susan Barington-Brown, minus $61\frac{1}{2}$.

"Fifth tied, Christopher Minton and John Manners.

"Seventh, Dick Hayward.

"Eighth, June Cresswell.

"Will all those numbers come forward, please."

Captain Barton gave away the prizes and rosettes and the eight competitors felt rather foolish lining up to collect them without their horses. Henry was given a tiny cup as well as a red rosette, and Noel and Hilary were each given a medal with a horse's head on it. Susan had a green fourth rosette, and the other four all had white "very highly commended" rosettes.

Captain Barton told Henry that Echo was a very nice type of blood horse and just the thing for one day events, and Noel that she'd done very well, especially across country. He told Hilary that hers had been a good level performance, but not quite fast enough, and then he ran out of remarks, and just said "well done."

Henry said, "Do you think that we canter round on our feet?"

"No," answered Dick and John firmly. So Henry led the way out of the circle of clapping spectators at a sedate walk.

Mrs. Exeter, tall, dignified and dressed in the fashionable shade of carbon grey, was lying in wait for Noel.

"My dear, I think you're simply marvellous," she said. "I think they're both going beautifully. Tranquil always has been a pet, but Truant, well, he's a different story. But truly, I was flabbergasted. There he was sailing round looking every inch a Badminton horse."

Noel was overwhelmed by so much enthusiasm. "They're not going too badly," she said, "but of course they've improved a lot during the last week. The Major's helped tremendously."

Mrs. Exeter laughed. "You can't put *that* one across me," she said. "I know enough about riding to realise that a horse isn't made in a week. Have you chosen which you want to keep?"

"Oh yes, Truant, please. If that's all right by you," and Noel felt her legs go weak as she spoke. Supposing Mrs.

154

Exeter had changed her mind and wanted to keep Truant?

"But of course, my dear. Only it isn't the choice I expected. You're quite sure about it? You wouldn't like to think it over? So far as I'm concerned, Tranquil will be far the easier to dispose of, after all your work, I don't want you to regret your choice."

"No, I'm certain," answered Noel. "I like Truant much the best; he's so clever."

"Well, that's settled then. And I'll let you know about Tranquil's future. You won't want to keep him too long now with winter coming."

"Well, thanks awfully for letting me have them and for giving me Truant. It's terribly kind of you."

"Don't thank me. I can't thank you enough."

Muttering that she must see to the horses, Noel escaped from Mrs. Exeter, but she ran straight into the Major.

"Well done, Noel," he said. "That was a very good performance. You've certainly got a one day event horse there."

"He was awfully good," agreed Noel. "You really think I can do proper one day events on him? I'm old enough next year."

"Yes, but you'll have to improve your dressage."

"Yes, it's terrible," said Noel dismally.

"That horse doesn't use his hindlegs enough, but now your seat's improved you ought to be able to drive more. Trotting circles, that's the exercise for you."

"O.K.," said Noel. "I'll trot circles all through the winter, but anyway thank you very, very much for the course, and the one day event and everything—"

"Don't mention it," said the Major.

Christopher, who had been waiting impatiently, seized his opportunity. "I wanted to thank you too," he said, "for all you've done for us these hols. Considering you've been ill and everything, we've had a pretty good time. Though I wish we could have done the Pony Club competition."

"Well, there's still next year," said the Major.

"Yes, I must try to persuade my parents to buy me a horse—William's getting a bit outclassed and he's going on in years; it showed to-day—it's the first time he's ever been beaten by Wonder or Sky-Pilot."

"William's all right," said the Major. "It wasn't his fault you were beaten."

"I know you don't like the way I jump, but—"

"There's more to it than the way you jump," interrupted the Major. "Everyone's entitled to their own opinions, but to succeed a certain humility is necessary; one can't progress if one is already perfect."

"But I don't think I'm perfect," objected Christopher. "I know I've got faults, only—"

"That's all right then," said the Major, and he turned to Mrs. Cresswell who was hovering near.

"I do hope that you haven't over-tired yourself," she began fussily. "You've had such a long day. An early night and breakfast in bed to-morrow——you can't be too careful after the terrible time you've been through."

Major Holbrooke grinned. "My wife has extracted all sorts of promises from me," he said, "but I don't intend to keep them. What did you think of June?"

"Gracious me! I haven't recovered from it yet. So cool; uphill and down dale. 'Mummy,' she said to me, 'the Italian canter's the thing. I'm going to put Glory on the bit.' She's such a little thing, you wouldn't think she had it in her."

"You're quite happy then? I thought she'd come on a lot and that mare's jumping well."

"My gracious, yes. And now you've put her on the right road, June will put her back into it. You'll see. I know June; she's a worker."

Mrs. Exeter had spent a considerable time talking to Mr. Barington-Brown and now he called to Susan, who was watching them anxiously. "That's it then," he said. "You don't deserve him, but it's all settled and he is now yours."

"Oh, Daddy, thanks *awfully*," said Susan. "Goodness,

156

I never thought I'd have him. I liked him from the first moment I saw him," she told Mrs. Exeter.

"Go on then. Run along and tell your little friend," said Mr. Barington-Brown.

"Oh, Daddy, she's not little," said Susan, with a giggle; and then she turned and ran towards the stables, shrieking, "Noel! Noel!"

The other competitors were in the stableyard and Evelyn was holding forth.

"Those idiotic bonus marks. If you went that speed out hunting you'd be in front of the hounds *and* you'd wear your horse out in the first twenty minutes."

"Well, we b'aint hunting," observed Henry. "We be one day eventing, we be. And everyone knows that one day events are a training ground for the Olympic trials, so where does hunting come in? You're thinking of Hunter Trials."

"It's all wrong—" Evelyn began again.

"Go and tell the Major then," John interrupted. And Dick suggested, "Why not write to *Horse and Hound*?"

Susan said, "Noel, Daddy's bought Tranquil. Isn't it *simply super*?"

"Has he really? That's terribly good news. I was beginning to feel gloomy at the thought of him going."

"Can I fetch him to-morrow?" asked Susan. "Goodness, I feel excited."

"Some people have all the luck," said Christopher. "I wish my parents would buy me a horse."

The Radcliffes were saddling their ponies and the messengers fetched their mounts from the barn where they had been resting.

June rode into the yard on Glory. "Mummy's brought the trailer," she said, "but I said that I was jolly well going to hack home with everyone else."

"This all seems rather an anti-climax," observed Dick. "Have we all said our 'thank yous' separately? I don't feel that we ought just to fade away."

"What *could* we do?" asked John.

"Ride up and down the drive singing 'Auld Lang Syne'," suggested Henry in mocking tones.

"Yes," shouted everyone at once.

"As loud as possible," said Gay.

"At the tops of our voices," added James.

"All on horses," stipulated June.

"Come on, Henry. Come on, Dick. Up you get." Dick and Henry rode bareback and in headcollars.

They clattered up the drive, Marion singing tunefully but the others shouting as loudly as they could. They drew starts of horror from the Holbrookes' friends, who were gossiping over cups of tea or drinks. They sang "Auld Lang Syne" in the drive and again outside the front door, where they arranged the horses in a circle and cross hands. Then they gave View halloas and Henry borrowed one of his uncle's horns and blew, quite efficiently, the long sad strains of the gone to ground. They said good night and thank you to the Major, who had appeared at the front door.

They parted in the drive, riding away in two cavalcades, and, as the sound of hoofs grew faint, peace returned to Folly Court. The white house, the park and the harvested fields grew quiet in the fading light of the September evening.

JOSEPHINE PULLEIN-THOMPSON

SIX PONIES
PONY CLUB TEAM
ONE DAY EVENT
PONY CLUB CAMP

Meet the members of the West Barsetshire Pony Club and read about their riding adventures and hilarious escapades in four favourite books by Josephine Pullein-Thompson.

SIX PONIES

The Pony Club members face the exciting challenge of breaking in six New Forest ponies – and Noel earns a pony of her own.

PONY CLUB TEAM

The Major makes a bet that his team will win the Pony Club Hunter Trials, and runs a special training course for them. But with the Trials only a few days away, their riding is still hopeless . . .

ONE DAY EVENT

A great day for the Pony Cub – and Noel is determined to prove that Sonnet is good enough to win . . .

PONY CLUB CAMP

It's the high spot of the summer – as children and ponies arrive in glorious confusion at Folly Court to begin a week in camp. And there are some exciting surprises in store for them . . .

Armada

has a whole shipload of exciting books for you

Here are just some of the best-selling titles that Armada has to offer:

- **Gallop to the Hills** Patricia Leitch 50p
- **A Devil to Ride** Patricia Leitch 50p
- **Ponies in Peril** Diana Pullein-Thompson 50p
- **Jackie on Pony Island** Judith Berrisford 60p
- **Six Ponies** Josephine Pullein-Thompson 60p
- **Plenty of Ponies** Josephine Pullein-Thompson 60p
- **Armada Horse & Pony Quiz Book No. 2** Charlotte Popescu 45p
- **Stolen Ponies** Christine Pullein-Thompson 50p
- **Black Beauty** Anna Sewell 50p
- **Zoo Quiz Book** Gill Standring 45p

Armadas are available in bookshops and newsagents, but can also be ordered by post.

HOW TO ORDER

ARMADA BOOKS, Cash Sales Dept., GPO Box 29, Douglas, Isle of Man, British Isles. Please send purchase price of book plus postage, as follows:—

    1—4 Books .... 8p per copy
    5 Books or more .... no further charge
    25 Books sent post free within U.K.

Overseas Customers
    1 Book: 10p. Additional books 5p per copy

NAME (Block letters)

ADDRESS

While every effort is made to keep prices low, it is sometimes necessary to increase prices on short notice. Armada Books reserve the right to show new retail prices on covers which may differ from those previously advertised in the text or elsewhere.